THE GENERAL

KARLLUDWIG OPITZ

THE GENERAL

Translated from the German by

CONSTANTINE FITZGIBBON

THE JOHN DAY COMPANY *New York*

FIRST AMERICAN EDITION, 1957

Library of Congress Catalog
Card Number: 57-5983

Agamemnon is a fool to offer to command Achilles; Achilles is a fool to be commanded of Agamemnon; Thersites is a fool to serve such a fool; and Patroclus is a fool positive.

WILLIAM SHAKESPEARE, *Troilus and Cressida*

IT WAS raining.

The trees were dripping, the roads sodden, puddles everywhere. The men hoisted the coffin on to their shoulders and we marched off.

The path zigzagged up the hill behind the cemetery chapel. There were box trees. Marble angels hung their heads and gazed down sadly upon the graves. It was easy to see which of the dead had been a poor devil in his lifetime; his place would be marked with a cross, made of tin or maybe wood, while the rich had arranged for several tons of bronze or granite to be put on top of their corpses.

We had unfurled our umbrellas and now we clambered up the hillside. The rain poured down upon the flowers and the wreaths on top of the coffin. It trickled down the black overcoats of the undertaker's men.

I was right at the end of the cortège.

I was suffering slightly from heartburn, and l had to belch. Colonel Olten, who was walking immediately in front of me, turned round and gave me a surprised look.

I felt sorry that I had had to break his train of thought, doubtless devoted to the general who lay within the coffin. But I'd eaten a gherkin salad for lunch and my stomach was having a hard time coping with it. We were walking along a narrow path, past a font. A ragged hedge hid a mound of faded wreaths and dying flowers. Among them rusty tins were scattered, and broken vases. A little farther on was the old graveyard, which was being dug up. Weatherbeaten headstones flanked the path. There was a wooden box, full of old bones, and beside it another, containing young plants.

We climbed some steps, tramped down into a hollow between the sodden trees, then there were more steps to climb.

I thought: the general has turned his funeral into a tactical exercise without troops. Even though he's a corpse he can still muck us about. There were all sorts of marvelous spots in this cemetery which he could have chosen to be buried in.

There were perfectly suitable plots available just inside the entrance. But of course the general had to choose a place right on top of the hill to leave his bones. Maybe he wished to offer an impressive view to anyone who might visit his grave? Or was it because his wife was already buried up there? Who can say?

At last we'd arrived.

The hole in the ground was decorated with pine boughs, and the undertaker had thoughtfully laid down boards, so that our shoes shouldn't be too badly muddied by the damp and sticky clay.

The men lowered the general's corpse. The funeral

party moved closer together beneath their umbrellas. Every face was solemn.

"In the name of the Father, and of the Son . . ." the clergyman began to intone.

I stole a glance at the adjoining tomb, which was that of the general's lady. ELEONORE VON PUCKHAMMER NÉE VON FRABIAN was carved upon the stone lid, together with dates of birth and death.

I'd heard tell that the general's lady had been a good woman. I could well believe it. Twenty-five years of married life with the general must have required great firmness of character, to say the least.

The chaplain, in a few well-chosen words, was telling us what a fine fellow the general had been. "God, our Father in Heaven, we confide into Thy hands the spirit of this warrior who has now passed on." That's what he said.

A proper eye opener for the Almighty, I thought.

"We humbly beseech Thee to remember the burdens which he shouldered throughout the war years, the privations which he underwent, the wounds he suffered, the sacrifices which he endured in the defense of his fatherland," the clergyman's voice intoned. "O Lord, he was a soldier from the bottom of his heart."

Colonel Olten smiled and nodded. He was standing beside the general's daughter and he held his umbrella so as to shelter her from the rain.

There were not many people gathered about the grave. A handful of relatives, a scattering of friends. People who had known the general and who felt in duty bound to attend his funeral.

I thought: in the old days there'd have been a proper war dance around the general's corpse. Smoking catafalques, Chopin's Dead March, a guard of honor firing a last salvo, the clanking of spurs—oh yes, the graveyard would have fairly hummed. There'd have been well-turned orations: May he be enshrined in the memory of our race as a brave and outstanding officer, a true leader of men, a model of duty. That was the sort of stuff they would have spouted.

The clergyman was saying: "He chose a military career, for it was that that gave a meaning to his life. He died true to the oath which he had sworn before God and man. Let us pray: Almighty Father, everlasting God, in whose hands we are, in life as in death . . . ." We mumbled the words with him.

Then the corpse was lowered into the grave.

We threw earth and flowers on to the coffin, and I said: "God be with you!"

The general had vanished from my life. Now everything between us was over and done with.

The rain pattered against the top of my umbrella. It was cold and unpleasant. There was a smell of wet clothes, of graves. For a moment I contemplated two worms crawling excitedly over the heavy clay. Then I walked away.

I hurried down the path up which we had come. Between the graves, the trees, the bushes. And I thought about the general and about his life.

FIRST made the general's acquaintance on the day that he snapped at me:

"Horlacher, you're going to be my driver! Understand?"

I said: "Yes, sir."

"Get your gear together. And look lively about it, if I may say so," the general barked.

His pale blue, somewhat watery eyes were fixed on me. I felt as though I'd been whacked over the head.

My old top sergeant grinned as he wished me goodbye.

"I've chased you often enough," he said, "and it was my heartfelt desire that one day you'd eat a tin of rat poison and die. But as God is my witness I wouldn't wish this job of driving the general on my very worst enemy."

The top sergeant looked as happy as a sandboy.

"Keep your medals polished," he said, "and see you in the mass graves."

A ferocious-looking sergeant was sitting in the general's car, with a face to stop a clock and a bristly crew cut. The general stood beside it, chatting with his officers.

"Why does the old man want a new driver all of a

sudden?" I asked the sergeant, who was acting as temporary chauffeur.

"The old one let himself get caught playing kiss-in-the-ring with a female auxiliary on the general's staff, the silly idiot," he explained.

"Christ," I said. "Whenever a man comes a cropper in this life, there's always a piece of tail at the back of it."

The sergeant told me about the car.

"Engine's damn near had it," he said. "For instance when you put it in third you've got to keep your hand on the gearshift or it'll slip out again."

"Couldn't somebody find the old man a better crate?" I asked.

"This one has carried the general all the way through the war, so far," explained the sergeant. "It's the old man's charger, and knows his moods you might say."

"I'll make it neigh," I said.

That was my first mistake.

The general had finished his conference.

"God be with you," he snapped.

The officers clicked their heels and touched their caps. The general strode across to the car.

"I want Horlacher to drive me," he shouted. "Then I can see if he's any good at it."

I said: "Yes, sir!" and hoisted myself behind the steering wheel.

"Don't drive too fast," the general ordered. "It's a nice day today, and I want to enjoy the fresh air."

I thought, Well, well, well, and I started the engine. It gave a tremendous bang, and for a moment I imagined somebody had fired a pistol at me. Then the din became steady; it was as though some joker had tied a lot of tin cans to the exhaust. During the course of the war I had driven many weird and wonderful machines, but this one clearly took the biscuit.

A fine sort of sewage cart I'd inherited here. I'd get an ulcer driving a thing like this. That was dead certain.

"You've struck it lucky, getting the job of driving the old man about," the warrant officer at Division Headquarters announced.

He was a sergeant major and I was drinking a couple of beers with him in the mess. He must have weighed close on half a ton. The soldiers called him "Pigface." The name suited him. He wore a little row of decorations and a highly polished War Service Cross, First Class, with Swords.

I looked at it with some astonishment: "Are you that good?"

The sergeant major laughed.

"Here at Division we order them direct from the factory," he said. "Wholesale. Fifteen marks the hundredweight."

It was pretty quiet in the sergeants' mess.

A couple of female auxiliaries were lolling about.

"Nice bit of homework," said Pigface, ogling the girls. "The blonde one over in the corner, I can recommend her. Makes a first-rate little hot water bottle."

"Thanks," I said. "Playing about with little blue-eyed Christmas turkeys is the quickest way I know of slipping on a banana skin. Anyhow, the only thing they like about us is our pay."

Naturally enough I got to know the mess sergeant right away.

He was a silly old gaffer who had once been chef in a moderately good restaurant. He suffered from chronic eye trouble, which was why they'd shoved him into this cushy billet at Division.

"Slowly but surely this crowd is driving me round the bend," he explained to me. "These bastards carry on as though they were a bunch of belted earls! Nothing's good enough for them. One day the red wine's too warm, next day the white wine's too cold, or the meat's too tough, or there's too much vinegar in the salad. . . ."

"Relax, man," I said.

But the mess sergeant wasn't going to spare me any part of his lament. He had, as they say, buttonholed me. "And the worst of all are the ones whose wives feed them any sort of muck when they're back home," he went on, picking his teeth with the point of a table knife. "While the general hardly ever complains. There's nothing like a Prussian cadet school for bringing a man up proper."

"That's right," I said. "They give the boys toe rags to eat and bawl 'em out if they grumble. Which makes them damn easy to please for the rest of their lives."

We talked a lot of rubbish along these lines. I could almost smell the extra breakfast I was after, when suddenly the adjutant came sidling into the room.

He was a remarkable man, a recognized expert on wines.

A stirrup cup for the gentleman.

His face was crisscrossed with saber scars.

"Get out of here, you," he hissed at me.

It sounded like: We don't serve Jews.

God almighty, I thought angrily, the war's got us by the short hairs and a lousy false alarm like this jerk worries that I'm going to eat one of his lamb chops.

Funny habits they have at Division, I thought.

I crept into the map room.

I helped the lieutenants who were fixing bridges and

roads on the sand table. We traced rivers and streams through the sand and put model guns and model tanks in their right places. We'd only just finished when the adjutant came in, and after he'd sniffed about the place he ordered me to work the hands of the cardboard clock while the sand-table exercise went on. Not what you'd call an exhausting job.

At precisely 1400 hours, not a second early or a second late, the general stamped into the map room, followed by a group of officers.

He gave a critical glance at the sand table. Then he began his speech.

"If we should ever be forced to abandon our system of linear defense along the Channel coast, it is highly probable that the Army will form a hedgehog," he said. "All you gentlemen know the form from Russia. Briefly, a deep zone of demolitions and long-range artillery fire to break up the attacks which the enemy will mount. Intention is well known: the creation of suitable conditions for flanking operations by our mobile troops, compelling the enemy to canalize his movements within certain specified areas, the splitting up of the enemy's forces, and the covering of our own counterattack which is being mounted in our rear area. The division's task will be to move smoothly into the new sector assigned it by Army."

The general glanced sharply at the bored faces about him.

"Gentlemen," he said, "I would impress upon you that these sand-table exercises are a tedious but essential by-product of our service. There's one thing we all know: when the balloon goes up, if we don't know our jobs so thoroughly that we can give the necessary orders even in our sleep, then the division might just as well be written off."

The general raised his hand, summoning the officers to approach the sand table. He ordered Colonel Olten to start the exercise.

The colonel was G3 on the divisional staff. A lively fellow. Not overeducated. Always wore very beautiful boots.

The officers played the sand-table game with all due subtlety.

"Herr Bredwitz," the general asked the adjutant, "would you be so good as to tell me why you haven't pulled back Anti-tank Battalion 115 from the railway bridge?"

"Sir! May I report? The anti-tank gunners are there to cover the infantry," announced the adjutant.

"Don't set yourself up as guardian angel for the dog faces," growled the general. "Any infantry still on the far side at this stage can be regretfully written off.

Or do you imagine the enemy air will make us a present of the railway bridge?"

It did me good to see Bredwitz's sour expression.

A few minutes later a complete tank battalion was wiped on the sand table.

The general lost his temper and became extremely outspoken.

Quite right, I thought. Nice prospect for us, if these deadheads are allowed to pulverize our best troops just like that. Somebody should slap a prosecution for damages by negligence on the oafs, and confiscate their salaries.

But in that case of course they'd all be dead of hunger.

The general was checking up on the billets of the division. The little birds were all tucked up in their nests and we were flitting down the dark corridors of France.

In front a truck full of divisional brass, behind a jeep full of officers.

Somewhere beyond Fougères we found ourselves in an inky village. Only in the guardroom was there a welcoming light to be seen. There soldiers were lolling about, playing cards. It took some time before they realized what was up. A long drink of water of a corporal put his tin hat on top of his head and saluted.

"Jump about! Enemy airborne troops are reported in your village area," shouted the general. "Give the alarm!"

The corporal turned on his heel, and with impressive deliberation told one of the soldiers:

"Go and wake up the company commander."

"Give the alarm!" thundered the general.

"Get a move on," said the corporal to the private. "And while you're about it tell the top sergeant, too."

The general was flabbergasted.

"This is what you're supposed to do," he shouted, and seized a machine gun from the rack.

An officer rammed on a magazine; the general dashed out of the guardroom into the darkened village street.

He fired a couple of bursts.

The soldiers in the guardroom gaped at one another in wonderment.

"Someone gone mad?" yelled the sentry who was patrolling the street. "Firing off guns in the middle of the night! What the hell's going on here?"

He came running, furious.

When he reached the guardroom light and saw what was happening he began, in a frightened stammer:

"I thought . . ."

"You're not in the Army to think," snarled Bredwitz. "Give me your paybook."

"I've seen a lot in my time," roared the general. "But I've never seen so scruffy a collection of undisciplined hooligans as this little party. Never."

The village remained dark. Not a sound to be heard.

"Peace, perfect peace," grinned one of the officers.

"Please be so good as to spare us your unwanted comments," grunted the general.

Angrily he picked up the machine gun and fired another burst at the sky.

A half-dressed lance corporal came panting down the street.

"The sergeant major sent me. To find out what all this firing in the middle of the night is about."

The general rolled his eyes and let his jaw drop.

In the darkness someone belched.

Ten minutes later he was giving the sleepy company a going over to make your hair stand on end.

He had the soldiers crawling along the street on their bellies till their mouths were so full of good French dirt they'd never need to buy any more toothpaste for the rest of their lives.

Wonderful show he put on.

That was my general.

When he came across to the car I was standing stiff as a ramrod. I snapped open the door.

The general noticed the new wireless antenna which I'd rigged up the day before. He stopped.

"What's that?" he asked, a gleam of distrust in his eyes.

"So that the general can listen to the Armed Forces communiqué while on the move," I explained.

For a moment he stared at it, with harmless interest. Then he drew in his chin and hissed:

"You will remove this piece of nonsense at once. What on earth do you think you're up to? Who told you you could start rebuilding my car? I suppose you're planning to install a flush toilet next?"

Hold on to your hats, boys, I thought, this is it.

The general shuffled around the car, inspecting it from every angle.

"What's this thing?" he asked.

"Those are the fog lamps, sir," I said.

"They're coming off too," the general ordered. "If it's foggy you can oblige me by opening your eyes a little wider."

"Yes, sir."

"And what the devil is this?" the general asked with astonishment, eyeing the little flag on the front of the car.

"Your new standard, sir," I reported.

"What's happened to the old one?" he asked.

"I burned it, sir. The flag was all torn."

The general swallowed a bellow of rage.

"Bredwitz, did you hear the monstrous thing the man said?"

The adjutant was temporarily deprived of the powers of speech.

"That standard went through the Polish campaign," the general began at the top of his voice. "I took it with me through Holland, and Belgium, and Russia."

These are details which I could willingly do without, I thought.

"In the name of all that's holy, are you totally lacking any grain of common sense? I suppose if you had your way you'd send the flags from Torgau and Leuthen to the laundry and then give them a good ironing, you numbskull. You'd cover Alexander the Great's battle monuments with a nice new coat of chromium. Good God!"

The general had his say.

He was so angry he could have cracked Brazil nuts between his molars.

He had hardly sat down in the back seat before it started all over again.

"What's the meaning of this thing?"

"It's a flower vase, sir."

"A WHAT?" shouted the general. "You mean it's

for me to put my posies in—when my regimental
commanders give me bunches of forget-me-nots? How
about an umbrella stand, and a peg to hang my top hat
on? The parlor maid and the footman you've tucked
away under the mudguards, I suppose? All you've got
to tell me now is where you've put the enema, and I'll
be happy."

It was endless, till at last he'd worked it out of his
system.

He showed his teeth like a watchdog chained up in
a farmyard.

There was nothing I could do about it. I couldn't
even clout him one. He was my general.

The next unit we visited was an assault gun battalion. He said to the C.O.:

"Tell me, my friend, have you got any practice
ammo on hand?"

"Yes, sir, I have," replied the simple-minded battalion commander.

"Good. Then let's assume that enemy airborne
troops have holed up in the farm buildings over there,"
the general said. "Show me how you'd get them out if
this were the real thing."

Soon assault guns were rumbling through the darkness, among a roaring of engines and a clatter of
tracks.

The guns thundered, the machine guns spat fire.

I observed the general who was standing a few yards in front of the hood, attentively watching the assault guns lumbering about in the night. I don't know, I thought, whether it'd really suit me to be a general, on the move the whole damn time. Not my sort of thing, come to think of it.

"Horlacher, I'm taking a few days' leave," said the general.

I was so amazed that I answered as though I were a human being.

"Really?" I said, in a friendly voice.

The general had a shack in the Black Forest. His daughter kept house for him.

I made the necessary preparations for the trip.

The general sat beside me. He looked at the countryside, which he knew. He knew it well, from the First World War.

"France has changed a great deal," he said. "It's become more beautiful, but it's aged as well. It has had to swallow a great deal of blood and iron."

"Seems to agree with it, though," said I.

We drove across France, along narrow roads flanked to left and right with slender poplars. We were crossing a rolling landscape and from each hilltop we had a wide view of the countryside.

"In the last war a million men died hereabouts," said the general, and he peered out at fields and meadows.

"On the French side, four hundred thousand, and the bodies of three hundred thousand of them were never found. That will give you a rough idea of what the artillery was like in these parts."

A cow, frightened by the car, galloped clumsily across a field.

Once there was a rotted tree stump close to the road. A little farther on I noticed a rusty angle iron.

"Funny the way there's nothing left to see of it all," I said.

"Yes, there's nothing left to see," said the general. "But the potatoes they grow here have a horrible taste of T.N.T. to them."

There are worse things they could taste of, I thought.

"What is in those boxes?" the general's daughter asked. She was a high-class piece of goods and waggled her behind.

"Souvenirs from France, miss," I said. "A small contribution to the general's household."

The general's daughter stared at the lovely things. There was a greedy look in her eyes.

"Do you mean to say these sort of things are so easily come by in France? Well, they certainly can't complain that they're badly treated under the German occupation."

"They don't," I said.

"Horlacher, I wanted to ask you . . ."

"Yes, miss?"

"Could you get me this sort of thing often?"

"Willingly," I said. "If you'd like to make a list of what it is you want."

"And stockings?" she asked.

"Of course," said I.

"I take size 42," she whispered.

I suppose everybody's got nerves, after all. I grinned politely and helped with the unpacking.

"I'm so glad my father has got a sensible driver at last," she said excitedly. "Just imagine, your predecessor drove a dustcart in civilian life."

In the evening the guests came.

All people with decent names.

There was the garrison commander, an honest type, with his wife. She wore a magnificent evening dress and screeched in it like a peahen that has been in collision with a bicycle.

Then there was the director of the theatre in the nearby town, which was closed at the time. He was six foot four inches tall and looked like a collection of fishbones dressed up in a flapping suit of shoddy.

A professor came, who appeared to be in a daze. He was an old dodderer who did research into heredity.

"I came across a most interesting case recently, the parents showed strong recessive characteristics. The child . . ." he bleated at me, until suddenly he realized with a start that I was only the general's driver. Whereupon he turned toward the general's daughter.

During dinner the wife of the garrison commander remarked:

"He has said that in this most momentous battle of all history we cannot expect providence to make us a present of victory."

"He spoke the truth," said the theatre director.

"Absolutely correct," grunted the professor.

"Every man will be weighed in the balance, and he who has been found wanting must fall," said the garrison commander's wife. She spoke with closed eyes and an expression of supreme satisfaction.

The woman talked and talked. She did not apparently even need to stop for breath. She must have done a course for cloakroom attendants, I thought.

"The Almighty will be a just judge, that's what he said," she went on.

"God is, after all, comparatively reliable, if you

see what I mean. Don't you agree?" asked the professor.

"Our task, he said, is to do our duty as laid down by the Creator of the universe in accordance with the rules of the struggle for existence, so that we must not spare a single life if it be necessary in the interest of saving the life of the German people," the garrison commander's wife went on. "The Greater German Reich will arise from the sacrifices of the fallen, that was what he said," she went on breathlessly.

"Good health!" said the theatre director, his voice pulsating with emotion. He raised his glass and began to drink enthusiastically.

"Horlacher, a few more braised onions," ordered the general.

I served them to him and I watched while a piece of calf's liver was thrust between his teeth.

The general's daughter sat bolt upright at her end of the table. Her elbows rested lightly upon the edge. Distinguished and reserved, with eyes half closed, she picked at the food upon her plate.

I enjoyed looking at the general's daughter. Marvelous breasts. Varnished fingernails and red hair. High coloring. Eyebrows that went up a bit at the corners. Beautiful, arrogant eyes she had, too.

After dinner the gentlemen played cards and the

ladies poured all sorts of liqueurs down their throats.

They indulged in speculations as well.

"Why have we suddenly let the Russians take Orel and Kursk and Kharkov?" asked the garrison commander's wife. "Our soldiers have retreated right across the Dnieper! Why? That's what I'd like to know."

"I can't tell you," said the general's daughter. "All I know is that this war in Russia will be decided one way or the other."

"Pray God that He will grant us the victory we deserve," whispered the elder lady.

The general's daughter smiled.

"God works in a mysterious way," she said.

"We'll give them a lesson they won't forget in a hurry," maintained the general. "There are sixty divisions along the Atlantic Wall already. We'll make them jump about all right."

"And apart from that there are one or two nasty little surprises in store for the mob on the other side," said the garrison commander. "I've heard say that what our backroom boys are up to in Peenemunde is really astonishing. Rockets, you know, and all sorts of other novelties."

"God Almighty, when will the peoples of Europe finally realize that there is no nation in the world with so profound and honorable an understanding for the needs of western civilization as we Germans?" said the theatrical director. "With a little perception and sense this war could so easily have been avoided. Instead of stabbing us in the back, all Europe could have marched shoulder to shoulder with our soldiers against the Bolsheviks. One day Europe will bitterly regret this opportunity missed."

"That is a battle our children will have to fight," said the professor.

The garrison commander then related an anecdote concerning a cavalryman who had groomed his horses with such remarkable thoroughness that he had killed two of them thereby in the course of his military career.

Late that night I lay on my bed thinking about this and that.

I smoked and dozed.

Somewhere in the house there was the sound of bath-water running away, and a warm breeze coming through the open window stirred the curtains.

What do you want with a guitar? The general's daughter had asked me that afternoon when I was unpacking the thing.

I like to strum on it now and then, I had replied. But it won't worry you. I'll take it off into the woods or some place.

Why be so exclusive? the general's daughter had asked me. I'm fond of pretty little songs too. For instance: Then said the Princess Isis, the sort of man I like is . . . There had been a definite tone in her voice as she hummed it.

When she came into my room I noticed that she had painted her lips a little too brightly. She wore black patent leather slippers and her green nightdress was thin enough for me to see the gleaming whiteness of her hips.

I held out the packet of cigarettes and gave her a light. She inhaled the tobacco, puffing rapidly.

She blew the smoke in my face.

You wait, I thought. Once you've done a bit of moaning, and sobbing "Darling," you'll drop all those fancy airs.

The telephone rang.

Division Headquarters was on the other end of the wire.

The general thrust out his lower lip, hung up the receiver and gazed at me in silence for a moment or two.

"Horlacher," he said, "we're leaving. Seventh Army has ordered general alert."

We set off, flat out.

We wasted no time at all. All the same we arrived

too late. The Allies had landed at dawn. Precisely in the division's sector.

The sledge-hammer had come down right on top of our heads.

A VERY good German morning to you," I remarked to Pigface.

He was thumbing through a leather-bound notebook.

"Now's our chance to collect a couple of really decent decorations," I said.

"The Allies will throw a party for us to make your eyes pop out of your head," he remarked.

"Remains to be seen," I said. "Meanwhile I'm hanging up my bowels in the clothes cupboard."

The general immediately settled down to his professional duties.

I brewed him a particularly strong cup of coffee.

"They've got all sorts of gadgets and they're landing in swarms," reported Colonel Olten. "Amphibious tanks and landing craft and commandos and heaven knows what-all. The picture is that American airborne troops have come down north of Carentan and the English northeast of Caen. They're after the town, but 716 is standing fast and fighting well. Three hundred fifty-two has bumped the Americans near Vierville. Our tanks are ready to go, but Army won't give the order for the attack."

"Bloody marvelous," said the general. "It all depends on our defeating the invasion within the first forty-eight hours. If we don't manage to do that, we're lost because we've got no operational reserves," he announced. "All the reserves are in Russia, which is where they'll stay. How about the Panzer Lehr Division and the 12th S.S.? Everything back of the coast must be brought up and pronto."

"Get a link to Army," Olten ordered the radio officer.

"I hope you'll be able to find out what their game is," said Olten. "All they said to me was that the German High Command is sending us a thousand jet planes and forty U-boats."

"What next!" exclaimed the general. "I didn't even know our jets were developed that far."

"If they were to make their first appearance here it would be fine," said Olten.

The general spent some time deciding which of the cigarettes in his case he would smoke.

I unpacked his gear and ran him a hot bath.

Next day I drove the general to the front. Behind Mortain we met our first bomb craters. The roads were destroyed, and there were corpses and smashed vehicles everywhere. From time to time we saw a German supply column creeping cautiously forward through the bocage country. A few ambulances were headed inland. American fighter-bombers whined and screeched overhead.

Between the Vire and the Orne the scenery changed. There were ships far out at sea, peppering the fields and meadows with their shells. Bombers unloaded their cargoes. On both sides the artillery pounded. I stopped the car in the shelter of a thick hedge, and the general and his adjutant turned their field glasses up to examine the bombers: the planes came from England, turned in a great curve over Normandy, and laid their eggs.

"Mass production jobs," said Bredwitz in a tone of contempt.

The general lowered his binoculars and blew his nose.

"Horlacher, give us something to eat," he ordered. I opened the boot and pulled out the picnic basket which was inside.

There was cold roast beef and a bottle of fairly good red wine. I gave the cutlery a quick rub over and served the meal. Unfortunately there were no napkins.

It was a hot day. The corn was ripening in the fields. The grass and the fruit trees smelled sweet. Far away shells were exploding. Bombs crashed down and butterflies fluttered in the breeze. Up in the blue sky the planes' machine guns rat-a-tatted. Their engines roared murder, and swallows swooped on flies.

A curious noise made us all look up. A narrow burning streak was being drawn across the sky. It became steadily darker, and wider, and longer. A great flaming ball appeared which went: Boom! Tattered black objects trailing dirty smoke fell to the ground.

"Horrible!" said the general. "To be blown up together with a couple of hundred gallons of gasoline is a quick death, sure enough, but a damned unpleasant one all the same. What do you think, Herr Bredwitz? It must be remarkably quick, mustn't it?"

"I think so," said the adjutant. "The force of such an explosion is immense, and everything must be pulverized and burned within a fraction of a second. It's hard to believe that the nervous system could react at all within so small a period of time."

"Would the general care for another glass of wine?" I asked respectfully.

"Yes, yes, I should," he said. "And take a drop for yourself."

"Thank you very much, sir," I said.

I was much impressed because it was generally not the custom for a driver to be allowed to drink, particularly when there were senior officers about.

On the other hand we were parked fairly close to the front.

Under a bridge the commander of a tank regiment was waiting for the general.

This colonel was covered in mud from head to foot. He was a tough egg, who'd been through a lot at one time or another.

Instead of a tie he wore the Knight's Cross around his neck.

"Only four tanks left? That's a bad business. That's really all that's left of your regiment?" the general asked.

"Two seventy-fives are still worth taking back to the workshops," reported the colonel.

"That's chickenfeed," said the general. "I'm most upset."

He rolled his cigar thoughtfully between his fingers.

"I'll see if I can do something about it," he sighed. "I must find out where I can organize a few tanks for you."

"If I may say so, sir, make it German ones," the regimental commander said. "I really can't hope to do any good with old Belgian and Czech stuff when we're fighting the Americans and English."

"My dear friend, you're not telling me anything I don't already know," growled the general. "Do you imagine my point of view is any different from your own? If I'd had my way they certainly would never have been allowed to push all this captured junk into our hands. But unfortunately it wasn't for me to decide.

Indeed nobody cares what the generals want. There are too many of them. We've got more generals than Frederick the Great had privates."

The general's ears were turning pink with anger. An unexpected file of American fighter-bombers came screeching low above the road, shooting at a single lorry.

The general was disgusted.

"What sort of an idiot driver is that, to go joy-riding around here of all places?" he roared. "Must be a maniac," he bellowed, glancing at the lorry which was starting to burn among a cloud of smoke.

"General, do you see those planes?" shouted the tank colonel. "Those are the fighters with the damned rockets I sent in a report about."

"They really go right through armor?" the general asked incredulously.

"I'm sorry to say I can promise you they do," said the colonel.

"Well this is a fine how-do-you-do," murmured the general.

"And likely to get a lot finer," said the tank colonel.

The general brushed some dust from his trousers.

"My good friend," he said, "in the course of the coming night I'll send you some tanks, so that you'll be mobile again. It won't be many. Be careful with them, because they've got to take you down to the beaches."

"Yes, sir," said the colonel, and raised his hand to his cap.

"I'm really, honestly sorry that you should have taken such a pasting at the very beginning of the battle," said the general. "But you'll have a nice, sharp sword soon enough again, eh? And take a tip from me, don't go getting in the way of one of those rocket things. That's a really horrible invention."

From the foxholes, which were not too far away, came the rattle of machine-gun fire.

"It sounds to me as though you've got a customer in your shop," said the general.

"I'll go and see to him right away," said the colonel.

"Deal with him properly, so that he doesn't come snooping around these parts again in a hurry. Well, that's all for now. And God be with you, my friend."

The general walked slowly across to the car.

The command post of the infantry regiment was in a farmhouse.

Captured American, Canadian and English paratroops lounged about the yard, chewing their iron rations. German soldiers, back from the front, told about the fighting in the pillboxes along the coast.

In the kitchen the regimental commander briefed the general.

"During the night they shelled the coastal batteries. At first light an unusually heavy barrage was put down on the infantry and artillery positions. Almost at once amphibious tanks began to come ashore, also water-proofed vehicles, ack-ack guns, infantry guns and anti-tank weapons. Swarms of landing craft brought their assault troops to the beaches. Naval guns and rocket batteries destroyed our positions."

The infantry colonel was pale. Also he was sweating.

"If one's honest one must admit they really made a superb job of it," said the general. "Unfortunately at our expense."

"Their co-ordination was absolutely faultless," said the regimental commander. "What with the pillboxes being smashed and the ground absolutely ploughed up by bombs, I couldn't really put up any resistance worth talking about. Our sea mines and land mines had hardly any effect. They simply advanced straight through them, everywhere. If you ask me I think they've got some new trick for detonating mines."

"Amazing, all the stuff they've got. Almost makes you jealous," said the general.

There was a thunderous crash.

Plaster fell from the ceiling.

Window panes splintered and tiles slid noisily from off the roof.

"That's a very decent-sized gun they've got there," remarked the general.

"This is a filthy hole," said the infantry colonel. "They're potting at us all the time."

Officers of the regimental staff were standing about in the farm kitchen.

They said nothing, their eyes on the map which lay upon the table.

Flies buzzed.

The fireplace was full of dirty dishes. Pigs grunted in the byre.

"Well, well, so you've got pigs here?" asked the general.

"Yes, sir," said the infantry colonel.

"Put the creatures out of their misery before they die of fright from all the din!" said the general.

He stood in front of the battle map. In reality most of the lines and symbols shown upon the sheet were now nothing but piles of wreckage and corpses, out there in the country.

The officers craned their necks.

"In no circumstances must the enemy be allowed to enter Caen," announced the general. "Otherwise we'll be pushed straight back to the Loire. For the time being, Colonel, you must stay where you are. I'll help you as best I can. I think that the 1st S.S. Panzer Corps should begin to arrive during the coming night. Once they're here we'll be able to make things quite lively for the gentlemen on the other side."

The regimental commander stared at the battle map and bit his lower lip. He had dark circles under his eyes and his hands trembled.

"My friend, don't let it get you down, that's all I ask of you," said the general in aimable tones. "After all, we've still got the Fifteenth Army up in the north, haven't we? They won't just sit there and watch while we're put through the wringer. Tomorrow, or at latest the day after, the whole thing will have quite a different complexion. And when the replacements arrive you'll find you're in charge of a proper regiment once again."

There was a tremendous crash.

A fountain of earth shot up in front of the farmhouse.

Bits of hedge and foliage floated through the air.

Splinters of steel whistled about the place.

"Really most remarkable," said the general with obvious astonishment.

"Couldn't the mortar battalion at least do something for us?" asked the regimental commander.

"Sorry, I'm afraid not," said the general. "I need the mortars urgently somewhere else."

He walked over to the window.

The splintered glass crackled beneath his boots.

"Would you care for one?" said the general to the colonel, holding out his cigar case. "If there's nothing else I can do for you, at least I can offer you a smoke," he said, and he grinned.

French civilians were fleeing along the road in front of the farm.

With pushcarts and prams and fluttering tricolors.

The general observed them curiously. "What on earth these people think they're going to live on while they travel is beyond me."

The regimental commander shrugged his shoulders.

He didn't know either.

The mortars were on a path in the woods.

It was dark. Foxholes had been dug. Soldiers crouched in them.

"Less noise in the whorehouse!" growled the battery C.O., as I stopped the car.

The general did not give the young captain any time to make his report.

"I want you to pull out just as soon as you've finished firing," he said as he scrambled out of the car. "Apart from your people there's nobody left in the woods, is there? At least I hope not."

The general knew that the enemy range-finders

would very soon locate the mortars. It wouldn't be long before the enemy artillery replied to the mortar fire.

"The woods have been cleared of all other units, sir," reported the battery commander. "There are outposts at the end of the tracks, that's all."

The general nodded and smothered a yawn.

He ambled along the path with the captain. Behind them went Bredwitz and a young lieutenant from the mortars.

The general looked at his watch.

"Sixteen more minutes to go," he said. "Have you talked to Colonel Olten yet about your next job?"

"The colonel told me to report to him at nine o'clock tomorrow morning for orders," replied the captain.

"Really?" said the general. "Not till nine?"

He stopped and glanced down at the foxholes where the soldiers were awaiting their fire orders. Beside the mortars lay the ammunition for two salvoes. Everything was under control.

"There's still fourteen minutes to go, sir," announced the captain.

"Lovely night," said the general, gazing up at the sky. "Smells wonderful here," he said, and sniffed. "Rather like jasmine, don't you think?"

"Quite right, sir," said the captain. "It is jasmine. It grows wild over there, any amount of it."

"Really? That's most interesting," said the general.

"Surely that's unusual in these parts, isn't it? I'm extremely fond of jasmine. Last year my brother-in-law gave me two bushes. I didn't think the roots would take, but they've done remarkably well. They're at home, in my garden," said the general. Meanwhile he kept glancing into the foxholes.

Suddenly he stopped.

"Unless my eyes deceive me," he said, in a tone of disgust, "I think I can see a man smoking over there."

"Lieutenant, go and find out at once which of the men is smoking," the captain ordered sharply. The adjutant of the mortar battery disappeared hurriedly into the darkness.

"Whoever he is, he must be out of his mind," grumbled the general. "I could blow up with rage each time that I'm faced with such crass stupidity," he said. "They've no idea how far away a cigarette end can be seen at night. Gentlemen in the air force have assured me that one can spot such cretins from a quite incredible height."

"I'll see to it that the man is most thoroughly punished, sir," the battery commander assured the general.

"Yes, do that," grunted the general.

He glanced at his watch.

"Horlacher, go and fetch me a sprig of jasmine from the bushes over there. But naturally don't shine your flashlight. Understand?"

"Yes, sir," said I.

"This wild jasmine seems to me most curious," the general remarked to the officers. "I'd really like to know how it ever got here," he said confidentially.

Bredwitz and the mortar captain assumed expressions of intelligent understanding.

"Still nine minutes to go," reported the captain.

"Then it'll be your turn," said the general. "Give those Englishmen a couple of good bangs," he said. "And then, out of it as fast as you can."

The battery commander saluted and walked away.

The general and Bredwitz turned toward the car.

"You know, my dear Bredwitz, I've been mixed up in plenty of counter-battery concentrations in my time, God knows," said the general, "but so far as I'm concerned each one is always a most remarkable experience."

The general clambered into the car.

There was a dull rumble.

A whine, a howl, crescendo. One tremendous explosion succeeded another, till they became a single roar. Flaming comet-tails shot up above the wood. The mortar shells screeched through the trees, tearing off leaves and twigs. The blast flattened the grass and whipped up pieces of earth. A hissing, screeching, thundering pandemonium.

A mad caterwauling; with white and saffron lighting effects.

Suddenly all was silent.

Seconds later the sound waves of the exploding mortar shells reached us.

"I wonder what effect it had," said the general.

The mortars fired the second salvo.

I handed the general the spray of jasmine.

Before the enemy artillery had time to slice the woods into mincemeat, we pulled out.

During the drive the general explained to the adjutant that a first grade milch cow will eat, daily, at least ten pounds of good hay, approximately half that amount of oats, and with no trouble at all some fifty pounds of turnip. The general said: "As a supplementary diet I can't recommend soy beans too strongly."

I was ordered to take the general's better uniform and superior linen to his home. "Duckums, here I am," I said, by way of greeting, to the general's daughter.

"How's my father?" she asked.

I said: "Your old man can't bear the thought of leaving Normandy."

"Is that the way for you to speak of my father, your own general?" she screeched. "You ought to be ashamed of yourself. I won't allow it in my presence!"

"You know what I meant. Besides, my education wasn't quite as fancy as yours."

"Impudence," she muttered. "You ought to thank your God for allowing you to breathe the same air as my father."

"Let's drop it," said I. "It's not all gold that glitters out there, you know, and your old man isn't a particularly big cheese at that."

"His family were already tilling German soil when Henry the Lion was on the throne; at which time your ancestors were still hanging from their hands in trees," she said angrily.

"I'm not going to argue with you about that," I said. "Because I simply can't picture your lot down on their hands and knees digging the potato patch."

The general's daughter now started an ear-splitting squawk. It was easy enough to see she'd grown up close to the barrack square. She was so furious she couldn't stop about her ancestors and all.

"One Puckhammer fought at Zenta. Armed only with a club he smashed the skulls of nineteen Turks."

"Your family seems to be naturally aggressive," I said.

"You bloody peasant," she snarled, and then she spat.

"That's not ladylike," said I.

Her eyes narrowed and I could see she would willingly have dug her nails into my throat.

"In your whole wretched *life* you never so much as *dreamed* of having a woman with my background, if in a moment of complete *insanity* I hadn't fallen for your fancy tricks."

"You amaze me," I said. "Are you really such a collector's piece, or are you just putting it on?"

It was a question that was beginning to interest me.

It rained for a week and then the sun came out. A pleasant, friendly sort of day.

"The Americans are driving for Caumont," said Olten. "Now the fun will start."

"All the same," said the general, "the English aren't getting anywhere at Caen. Our division is as firm as a rock."

"I hope that won't land us in the soup," said Olten, pointing toward the battle map. "We're holding our sector all right, but how about our neighbors? Those gentry are beginning to get out faster and faster. We might as well write off this ammo dump, Bobby One, right away. I've laid on transport to pull as much stuff out of it as we can, but still most of it is as good as lost already." Olten stared at the map. "And we thought they'd never reach the dumps."

"Many a girl has set out on a pilgrimage and come home with a baby," grunted the general. He made a noncommittal gesture, then threw his pencil down on the table. "If it's going on this way, we might just as well ring down the curtain," he growled. He turned on his heel and gazed at the floor. "What's the sense in it? We sweat blood, we turn the whole world topsy-turvy, we sacrifice our tanks, and with what result? We lose our ammo dumps. And all because certain gentlemen don't know the difference between a yacht race and Wednesday, and what's more, won't learn. It's enough to make you tear your hair out in handfuls."

"You'll have to explain to Army what's happening, in words of one syllable," said Olten. "Why should we sacrifice our supplies for the sake of the other divisions? Incidentally, what I wanted to say: casualties have now reached forty per cent."

The general dug about furiously in his left ear with his little finger.

"That's wonderful," he said. "How long are we supposed to go on fighting with forty per cent casualties?"

"Yes," grunted Olten, "and that won't be the end of it either. We'll have to see if we can't somehow cut down our losses."

"By looking after our own affairs a bit more and other people's a bit less," said the general, and waved his hand.

"In that case what I propose is that we evacuate Bobby Two right away, otherwise it'll be the same snafu there."

"Right," said the general. "Let's have a look at the picture."

They both bent over the battle map.

"If they get Caumont, they'll get St. Lô, too," said Olten. "Once they're in St. Lô it's only a matter of days before the big round-up begins."

The general ran his finger underneath his collar and drew an audible breath.

An airplane raced over the roofs of the little town. The wind whistled at its passage. Rat-a-tat went the cannons in the wings of the plane. From far away came the roar of a quadruple flak gun.

The divisional supply officer entered the room. Quite a decent sort of family man, temporarily dressed up as a major.

"Come here," said the general, and pointed at the map.

"We've got to clear Bobby Two and in double-quick time before the lid snaps shut. Move the ammo here, between Falaise and Argentan. But for God's sake don't let your lorries block the Torigny-Mezidon road. I've got to have that kept clear. In fact keep off it altogether."

The puzzled supply officer stared at the map.

"General," he said, "if I'm not to use the road you say, how am I supposed to get from here to here?"

The major pointed at the map.

"What the devil are you talking about?" shouted the general, and his eyebrows shot up.

The supply officer clenched his teeth.

"So far as I'm concerned you can hire Chinese coolies and make them carry the ammo across the fields in baskets," snapped the general. "Good God, man, do you think I'm here to solve your transport problems for you? If you don't know how to do your own job, you'd better ask the local postman."

He was holding a magnifying glass. Angrily he threw it down on the map.

The supply officer gave a hurried and perfunctory salute, then vanished.

"That fellow's so stupid I'm surprised he remembers to blow his nose," muttered the general irritably.

He ran through the building, bawling out everyone he came across. He wrenched open doors, slammed them shut again, and tore such a strip off a harmless orderly officer whom he met in a corridor that the poor man thought he heard the last trumpet blowing.

"No harm meant, Olten old man," the general said, when it was all over. "From time to time I just have to blow my top, or I'd burst."

He folded his arms, like Napoleon.

"I know what you mean," said Olten with a grin. "Spiritual castor oil."

Pigface and I were enjoying a siesta. We leaned against the car and from time to time spat sideways on to the paving stones.

"The chaps up there are getting it hot," said the sergeant major.

"How did you guess?" said I.

"Aren't you glad now you got the job driving the old man?"

I said: "And how. Better than sitting in a foxhole with dirty fingernails."

"After the war they'll call us rear-area scroungers."

"We should worry," said I. "Think of all the medals we'll be able to collect!"

"On the Eastern Front," said Olten, "it's going from bad to worse. Orsha, Mogilev, Bobruisk lost, Third Panzer Army, Fourth and Ninth Armies torn wide open."

"It'll be the same story here," grunted the general. "We won't be able to hold Caen, despite all the men we've lost."

"We ought to withdraw to the Seine, join hands with Fifteenth Army and fight a mobile battle," said Olten. "Get the enemy on the hop, the way the Russians did with us in the east. That's the only thing which has any prospect of success."

"Rommel and Rundstedt have been ordered not to give up a single square yard," said the general.

"Gneisenau and all other saints," groaned Olten. "What next? Are we living in the Middle Ages? The enemy's intentions are perfectly obvious. A blind man with a stick could tell that they're planning to use Avranches as a pivot. If somebody doesn't get a move on, and damn quick, the Americans and English will be writing their own ticket. And then our boys in the Cotentin are in the bag."

The general lit a cigar.

"My dear Olten," he said, "I'm beginning to suspect that we've walked into a highly disagreeable rat trap."

"Your suspicions are likely to prove justified," remarked Olten sourly. The colonel walked across to his desk and thumbed vaguely through the sheaf of latest reports.

"Here in Normandy," he said, "it's a question of bending or breaking. Even a certified lunatic must surely see what will happen if the enemy breaks through to the east. The situation is critical, and the Fifteenth Army stands smartly to attention, miles away in the rear, practicing saluting by numbers! It would make you laugh if it weren't so sad."

"Send a telegram to Russia. Tell them to ship us a

hundred or two German divisions," growled the general between his teeth.

"Hell," shouted Olten, "if only we had them."

"Don't let it get you down, my friend," said the general. "Let's just take it as it comes."

"God almighty!" groaned Olten. "And the promises they keep making us!"

"Highly developed powers of imagination," muttered the general.

"What about the thousand jet fighters they were going to send us? What about that?"

"That was a flat and shameless lie," said the general.

"It's a bit thick," growled Olten. "I think our friends at High Command and all the other university graduates might have treated us a bit more handsomely. Why only one thousand? Why not ten? A few more one way or the other wouldn't have made any difference to the amount we actually got."

"My dear Olten, we shouldn't work each other up in this way. We've got enough to worry about as it is."

"I can't help it. This amateurish way of running a war is more than I can stand," shouted Olten. "What I'd like to know is where these dimwits got their military education, if any."

The general asked for a pernod. I brought it to him, also the carafe of water, which I placed beside the glass.

Bredwitz walked in. He was excited. He said:

"In Paris they've arrested the Gestapo. In Berlin the Guard Regiment is sealing off the government offices. At the High Command they're shooting staff officers."

The general sat down heavily in his armchair.

"There's talk that the Supreme Commander has been assassinated."

"I can't believe it!" whispered Olten in a shocked voice.

The general jumped to his feet.

"Get me a link with Army!" he bawled into the radio office.

"There's never been a rebellion in Germany, since Tauroggen, when General Yorck and his Prussians changed sides and fought against Napoleon. But that was necessary and historically justified, besides being in accordance with the real wishes of his King and supreme commander. True enough, our present commander is a man without any background or understanding of tradition, but all the same we've sworn an oath to him as the chosen leader of our nation, and that oath is no hollow formality."

"A day of shame," murmured Olten.

"Army on the line, sir," reported the signals officer.

"There's talk here of assassination of the Supreme Commander," the general shouted into the telephone.

His face was scarlet, his eyes fixed glassily on the wall map. He spoke only a few words. Then the conversation was over and he threw the telephone, which was still crackling, back on its cradle.

"Chief of Staff Commander-in-Chief West has been definitely informed by the head of the Organization Department at Army High Command that the assassination failed," he said. "The Supreme Commander is well and in good spirits."

He picked up a paper knife from off his desk and stared at it morosely.

"It's all absolutely insane," shouted the general.

"Mutiny and treason are always damned in the eyes of history, if the traitors don't carry out the job properly. To stab the Supreme Commander in the back at this decisive moment of the war is worse than rebellion, it's a crime."

"Well, thank God he's still alive," said Olten. "It's destiny."

"If God has granted our Supreme Commander His protection, it means that we are all the more deeply bound to him, and the German soldier has no choice save to follow him to victory in this war, or to defeat," said the general.

He picked up his pencil and his magnifying glass. He leaned over the map.

"Let us do our duty," he said.

Pigface had news.

"The Russkis have chewed up thirty German divisions," he said. "They're in Vilna. A couple of miles to go and the Moujiks will be over the border into East Prussia."

"Blow me down," said I.

"And here the Yanks are already in Rennes and Le Mans," said the sergeant major. "Cherbourg's cut off, and in St. Malo and in Brest and in Lorient and in St. Nazaire our chaps are being left to stew in their own juice."

"Look here, can't you think of anything more cheerful to talk about, man? Some people don't care for this graveyard stuff." I was angry. "What's for chow?"

"Bean soup, the life blood of the German fighting man," grunted Pigface.

The rumble of artillery was endless and steady. The bursting of the shells was like a winter thunderstorm. A lunatic screeching and roaring made all France tremble. The general was shaving. Then he drank his morning coffee and ate a light breakfast, an omelet.

The din of the guns reached its highest peak. The general carefully lit a cigar, and as he puffed out the first cloud of smoke, the infantrymen crept out of their foxholes and allowed themselves to be sliced into rashers by pieces of white-hot steel.

"God be with you," said the general as he entered the map room.

"A good morning to you," said Olten.

The general rubbed his chin and glanced at the glowing end of his cigar.

"I don't like the look of this attack," he said. "Threatened on three sides and then to thrust your head farther into the noose, doesn't make sense to me. No, I really don't like the look of it."

"If we'd had our way it'd have been a different story," said Olten.

"That you can be quite sure of," said the general.

"It would be a good thing if we were to get some idea of how we're going to pull what's left of the party out of the wreckage," said Olten. "Because there's going to be an encirclement. On the line Falaise-Mortain. My bet is that we'll have to get out by way of Rouen."

"That would be the best way," said the general. "Come, my friend, let's have a look at the picture."

He stepped across to the map table.

His brain began to work feverishly. Where were the survivors to go? And how about the guns? And the equipment? And the ammunition? And all the vehicles?

This attack would end in a disaster. The general knew it. Now he must work out everything; including thinking about the dead, which he wouldn't have under his command any more.

"Make arrangements for the headquarters to move!" he bellowed. "And the workshops are to go across the Seine at once," he ordered. "The railway bridge is still standing, I hope?"

"It's still standing," Olten replied.

The general peered at the map.

"First the tanks must go, bit by bit."

"And as quietly as possible," said Olten. "Or else Army will blow us up in no uncertain terms. Might I make a suggestion? Why not move them first of all to Falaise? Then we'll have them where we can lay our hands on them, and besides it'll make the order to pull out more comprehensible to Army."

"Do you think that the gentry at Army still have the faintest understanding of what's brewing hereabouts?" asked the general.

"Isn't it about time those strategic geniuses formed a hedgehog at last?" asked Olten.

"The devil alone knows what our masters have thought up for themselves," grumbled the general. "You know the old saying: whom the gods will destroy they first drive mad."

He was drawing on the map with his pencil.

"And we'll bring the assault guns back out of the danger area too, quietly of course," he ordered, marking their new position on the battle map. "The infantry will have to carry back the can, as usual, but unfortunately there's nothing I can do about that."

"Orderly officers!" Olten bawled into the next-door room. "Assault Gun Battalion 3 to go to Argentan at once," he said to one of them.

"My friend, have you any ideas about extricating some of the infantry when Tank Regiment 101 moves out?" the general asked. "They're having a damned hard time, the handful of them that are left."

Olten glanced at the map. "It's hard to see where we could take them from," he said. "Though I don't see why the tanks shouldn't pick up the stragglers."

The general thought about this.

"Yes, by God, let them pick up the odds and ends," he ordered. "And lay on reception points."

"Orderly officer!" Olten yelled into the next-door room. "All stragglers and walking wounded together with tank crews and truck drivers without vehicles, in fact all men that can still shoulder a musket to assemble at once in St. Quentin!"

"See a copy goes to Field Police," shouted the general. "And I want short shrift for shirkers found sneaking off. There's no point in wasting time with those fine fellows."

This was the sort of job the general loved. Drive; no beating about the bush; the general was happy. He was in his element. This was his profession. The marks on the map multiplied.

The new positions arose visibly with the movements of the pencil.

The general was doing what he wanted with his own division.

"I'll lay you even, by day after tomorrow the pincers will have met between Falaise and Argentan. Taken?" he asked.

"It'll be an astonishing spectacle if they do," prophesied Olten.

The tip of the general's forefinger followed the line of the Seine along the map.

"Here," he said, and tapped the map. "Sotteville, that's the crossing place for us. That's the hole in the bag."

"Get on to the Navy and order two flat-bottomed boats!" Olten shouted through the open door. "To be delivered at Sotteville," he added loudly.

"Once we're over the river we'll assemble the tanks in front of Amiens and the supply echelons in the Beauvais area," the general ordered. "There's gasoline for them there."

Thus did he rap out a long sequence of orders.

The divisional staff cursed and grumbled under the work which the general thrust upon the officers.

The general slaved away. Sweat poured from him, nor did he let up for a single minute.

"Do you know, my dear Olten," he said, "I don't think we should praise ourselves, but it's on occasions such as this that one sees whether a man really knows his job and can really control events."

"Almost a platitude, what?" said Olten. "But true enough all the same."

They gazed into one another's eyes. And they saw, reflected, profound mutual admiration.

The general climbed into his camp bed.

He read the Bible for a minute:

And her daughters which are in the field shall be slain by the sword: and they shall know that I am the Lord. For thus saith the Lord God, Behold, I will bring upon Tyrus Nebuchadnezzar King of Babylon, a king of kings, from the north, with horses, and with chariots, and with horsemen, and companies, and much people. He shall slay with the sword thy daughters in the field: and he shall make a fort against thee, and cast a mount against thee, and lift up the buckler against thee. And he shall set engines of war against thy walls, and with his axes he shall break down thy towers. By reason of the abundance of his horses their dust shall cover thee: thy walls shall shake at the noise of the horsemen, and of the wheels, and of the chariots, when he shall enter into thy gates, as men enter into a city wherein is made a breach: With the hoofs of his horses shall he tread down all thy streets: he shall slay thy people by the sword, and thy strong garrison shall go down to the ground. And they shall make a spoil of thy riches, and make a prey of thy merchandise: and they shall break down thy walls, and destroy thy pleasant houses: and they shall lay thy stones, and thy timber, and thy dust, in the midst of the water.

The general derived great edification from his Bible-reading.

Meanwhile I was putting out clean linen and fixing a new blade in the general's safety razor so that he might shave off the stubble on his chin next morning.

It was then that the first bombs fell.

To begin with I thought it was a mistake. I believed it was an accident. Divisional headquarters was in an old château, surrounded by thick woods, and the trees hid the building. Maybe a bomber on the way home was simply unloading its eggs here because it had to get rid of them somewhere or other? That's what I thought.

There was an uncommon loud noise and the house began to shake. The lights went out. The rest of the stick was already crashing down in the woods. People were running down corridors and through the hall in panic. Some were bawling orders. Others went helter-skelter down the stairs. In the darkness they tripped over one another, treading on faces or backsides. Pieces of furniture toppled over. Windowpanes splintered. Plaster fell from the ceiling. On the walls pictures and maps danced a jig.

"Are you still there, Horlacher?" the general asked.

I am for the moment, I thought, but I don't know for just how long. I leaned against a wall, swallowing pulverized plaster. The glass tinkled from the windows and the blast sucked out the curtains. There were flames outside. In the woods trees split and crashed.

"Bound to happen sooner or later," said the general, as he sat down on the edge of his bed.

"They got us this time," said I.

Bombs of all shapes and sizes screeched and screamed and whistled down. Where they landed they tossed fire and earth and bits of trees high in the air.

"We're just as likely to catch one in the woods as we are here in this room," said the general.

I thought: keep your trap shut, I'm saying my prayers.

The bed, the cupboard and the table lurched and swayed as one explosion followed another. The general sat there quite calmly, gazing through the broken window. He was leaning forward, and I could clearly see his bald pate shimmering in the light of the flames.

Bredwitz was struggling through the filth and debris which blocked the hall. He stopped in the doorway: the door had been torn from its hinges, "Excuse me, sir, it's about the flak. You said it was to go forward, but you didn't say where exactly."

The general sighed.

"Ah yes, my dear Bredwitz. When Marius fought the battle of the Raudian Plains he was luckier than us. All he had to deal with was Teutonic war hounds. Those were the days."

He dressed carefully and then went down into the cellar with the adjutant. Back to work.

Hand grenades landed among the leading elements of the division. Tommy guns stuttered from the roof-tops. Mines were thrown down into the street. Trucks began to burn. Wounded soldiers ran along the house fronts.

"Partisans?" the general asked.

He drawled the word, very slowly.

"We ought to by-pass the town," said Olten.

"No, we shan't do that," grunted the general. "We'll drive slap through the middle of the place. The tanks will give us covering fire. Put the soft-skinned vehicles in the middle. Tanks in front and at the back. Then I'd like to see if these Frenchmen will have the guts to spit on our heads."

"I suggest we avoid mixing it with the Maquis," said Olten, whose mind was made up.

"No, my friend," murmured the general. "What on earth has happened to us to make us scared of these Frogs and their Ku-Klux-Klan?"

The division drove through the town. The shutters were down in front of the shops. The cafés were crammed with Frenchmen, behind drawn curtains.

It was just as the division's supply lorries were crossing the square in front of the railway station that the shooting began.

I was driving the general's car immediately behind a quadruple flak gun. It fired all four barrels into a hotel. Windowpanes and stucco and flower pots crashed down into the boulevard. Machine-gun bullets rattled through the glass front of the station. It splintered and smashed. Somewhere indoors a woman was screaming shrilly. Kids were bawling. A group of Frenchmen came running out of a doorway. The grenades got them and they spun like marionettes until they collapsed on the pavement. Tommy guns were spattering bullets from a cinema roof. Four men and one woman were crouching behind a chimney pot. The quadruple flak gun knocked them off like so many lame sparrows.

I snatched my sub-machine gun and began to fire eagerly.

The general, who was seated beside me, pointed out suitable targets.

The captured Maquis were tried by a drumhead court-martial. There were seventeen men and two women. They sat in a school classroom, waiting. Soldiers stood around, glaring at them angrily.

"You wait, you bastards. We're going to bloody well tear your guts out."

"This is the old whore what did in Fatty Heinrich in the Second Battalion. I saw it myself how she shot him, the bitch."

"You goddamned swine."

"What's the sense in giving them a trial?"

"It's all got to be done proper and regular," Pigface explained to the privates. "So as this time they won't be able to say we acted like Huns when we was in their country."

"They'll say that anyhow," said the men, and grinned.

"I'll have the little tart up front there," said one soldier.

"She's the one what threw the grenade into the field cooker. Killed two and spilt all the beans."

The girl was a miserable young thing. She wore a shabby pullover and no stockings.

"Listen, ducks," I said, "this soldier here wants to lay you afterwards."

"*Oui, Monsieur,*" she said and looked at the soldier from head to toe, her expression one of loathing and contempt.

Then she spat in his face. The men beat her up good for it.

The judge advocate opened the door.

"In here, you whore," he snarled.

"O.K., bitch, time to make your will," said a lance corporal.

"Oh, shut up," I said, "she doesn't understand what you're saying."

"That bloody cow killed my chum Fatty Heinrich of the Second Battalion."

"Hanging them's better than shooting," remarked a corporal. "I saw it in Russia. Really squirm about, they do, when you string 'em up."

"Ah," said I.

"I wish to see if they know how to die," the general explained. "Since they were so anxious to kill our men."

I helped him into his coat. We drove out of the town, and I stepped on the accelerator rather more firmly than usual.

A field policeman was guarding a crossroads. He gave a smart salute, exactly as laid down in the drill book, and we turned off into the side road.

They had dug a ditch, and an old man was cleaning his spade with a handful of turnip tops, while a young boy scraped the mud off his boots with a sharp stick. The two women stood off to one side, watching.

The lieutenant in charge of the firing squad hurried toward the general. The general waved him away. He did not wish to hear any report.

The lieutenant saluted and marched back to his original position.

"In groups of four," he explained in French. "With a final group of three," he added.

The soldiers collected the spades. The two women were the first to move across and stand in front of the hole in the ground. The men glanced at one another, uncertainly. They did not know who was supposed to go first.

"Come on, come on," said the lieutenant to encourage them.

The old man who had cleaned the spade went over to the trench. After a moment or two the boy began to follow him. He turned back and waved. While doing so he stumbled over a furrow. He shook his head in surprise.

When the four of them were standing in front of their grave, they sang the "Marseillaise." But only a couple of bars before the rifles crackled.

"Next, please," the lieutenant called in French.

Four men stumbled across the field in single file. They sang their national anthem, and one of them began to shout. "Fascist swine! Murderers!" he yelled, and raised his clenched fist.

The other three turned to look at him. At that moment the rifles fired again.

Why is this lieutenant in such a hurry? I wondered. Why doesn't he wait at least until the men are properly lined up? After all, they might like to shake hands or something, mightn't they?

"That tune, the 'Marseillaise,' quite fascinating, most catchy," said the general.

His eyes reminded me of a cat's, watching sparrows.

"They really do behave admirably," he said. "Are they not Communists?"

"Certainly, sir," said Bredwitz.

Once again the riflemen fired. The adjutant turned away and wiped his brow with his handkerchief.

"Filthy job this," growled the general. "Come along, Bredwitz, we'll go now."

I opened the door for them, before sliding in behind

the wheel. The general leaned back in his corner, and Bredwitz handed him the traveling robe, for it was a cold day.

Once again a salvo rang out and the rattle of rifle bullets drowned the thin singing of the few condemned who still remained alive.

I started the car.

"May God have mercy on them, the mercy which we could not show them," murmured the general, and he touched his cap.

He's got nice manners, I thought.

"Every step we take our flanks get longer and proportionately more dangerous," said Colonel Olten. "Another sixty miles and we're out of the Ardennes."

"Let's hope that this lousy flying weather goes on for a bit," said the general. "At the moment that's our only hope."

The general checked his map references.

"No telling what'll happen if they catch us in this impasse," he said.

"Yes, that would be a nice how-do-you-do," sighed Olten.

He walked across to his desk and fetched his cigar case. With care and attention he selected a dark Brazilian cheroot. He deliberately snipped off the end.

And while striking a match and inhaling the first puff, he gazed at the battle map.

"It is surely utterly basic that when carrying out such a maneuver as this the prime military condition must be to secure one's flanks," he said. "Why isn't it being done?"

"A spectacular example of total muddleheadedness," remarked the general.

"We're making it all so damnably easy for the gentlemen on the other side," said Olten. "They'll have plenty of time to accustom those long-service N.C.O.s of theirs to high command in action."

"Say that in America, and you'll be tarred and feathered," grinned the general.

Olten pointed at the maps.

"If our advance isn't covered with all speed here, and also here, they'll attack from the north and south and simply cut off our tail."

The colonel drew a couple of arrows with his pencil on the table.

"And when they do," he said, "there'll be so many people trying to get through all at once that it'll look like the entrance to hell."

The general laughed.

"Isn't there anything we can do on our own initiative to improve things?" Olten asked.

"This endless business of pulling other people's chestnuts out of the fire," said the general, and screwed up his face. "Besides, they'd say I'd weakened the attacking force and I'm not particularly keen to lay myself open to that."

"They could equally well say we hadn't disposed our forces properly," said Olten. "Anyhow why should you worry what these chair-borne strategists say?"

"I don't give a damn, as well you know," said the general. "But just for that reason I'm not going to stick my neck out for their sake. And in circumstances like these if I were to act on my own initiative that's exactly what I should be doing. After all, I'm not the field marshal, am I? Let him worry about how this business of ours is going to turn out. It's his headache, isn't it?"

"It doesn't look as though he's losing much sleep over it," said Olten with a sneer.

"God almighty, what can I do?" shouted the general. "Without any reserves whatsoever."

"We should at least send a few tanks over here," said Olten, pointing at the spot on the map. "Then we'll be able to pull our men out again when the fun starts, if the worst comes to the worst."

"My good friend," said the general with deliberate placidity, "it's always the same old story. Send troops into the attack and then sit back and wait for them to be cut off. You'd almost think somebody was devoting his entire energies to the destruction of the whole Army in double-quick time."

"That's precisely why it's up to us to act on our own initiative," grumbled Olten.

"Far too late for that sort of thing," said the general. "There's only one thing we can do now: play the game the way they want it played to the final whistle."

"Back home in the churches they're bawling about peace on earth and goodwill to men," Pigface moaned. "While here a hundred thousand soldiers march to the mass graves in columns of four."

"Yes," said I. "That's Christmas new style. What about the Teutonic Yuletide at which our forebears were accustomed to devour a succulent wild boar, crackling and all?"

"THE chips are down," said the general.

The staff officers and the surviving troop commanders were standing in the map room. Outside the building the snow was turning to slush and the woods were hidden by heavy fog.

"After these last battles we can hardly consider ourselves as a division any more," the general explained. "Therefore from now on we'll be called Battlegroup Theodor Körner."

The general strode up and down.

"You, gentlemen, will no longer command regiments, but units."

The general stuck his thumbs into the breast pockets of his tunic.

"The division still has at its disposal some eight hundred men. They'll be split up into four units. Weapons, ammo and equipment will be similarly divided. That also goes for the trucks and whatever fuel is still on hand. The staff company and the supply columns are dissolved and their men will be incorporated in the units. All superfluous baggage will be scrapped, ruthlessly. All gear we don't want will be disposed of to other units, against a receipt of course. Alternatively the stuff will be destroyed. After which, general withdrawal all along the line. The four units will be ready to march off by twenty-three hundred hours. The battle group is retiring into the Alpine Redoubt. Please don't ask me, gentlemen, what the Alpine Redoubt is, because I haven't the faintest idea. They have announced that the Alps are a redoubt, and for the time being that's all we know about it."

The general's thumbs emerged, twiddling, from under the lapels of his breast pockets. He hunched his shoulders.

"If I may ask a question, sir? I don't see how my tank crews can be expected to fight as mountain infantry," said a major.

His voice was chilly and very forceful.

"What are we supposed to be doing in the mountains?" he asked in the same tone.

"What on earth do you mean?" snapped the general. The corners of his mouth went down and he stared angrily at the major.

"How about the German civilian population down below? That's what I mean," said the major.

"In heaven's name, how am I supposed to know what's going to happen to those leather-trousered boobies?" snarled the general. "If this is the pay-off, they'll have to get used to it. After all, we can't evacuate half Bavaria. What's more, is it any business of yours? Your sympathetic feelings are doubtless highly creditable to you. But civilians on the other side of the frontiers have been through it all before now, haven't they? Well?"

"I don't like that man's attitude," the general explained, a few minutes later, to Colonel Olten. "An officer isn't supposed to have such idiotic emotions about civilians. Particularly in war time."

I took the general's valise to his daughter.

I arrived early one morning. The general's daughter was in her dressing gown.

"Well, how goes it, you old war-horse," she asked, looking at me intensely.

I said: "I've had a bellyful."

"I can see that," she said, and grinned. "Would you like a cup of coffee?"

"Afterwards," I said.

We kissed, and I thought: as a woman she's terrific.

"What's going to happen to us two?" she asked.

"I don't know," I said.

She looked at me, and the smile vanished from her face. Damn it, I thought, maybe the others aren't so coarse about it, but they do it just the same, and whichever way you slice it. . . .

"Now I'll make you a cup of coffee," she said.

"To hell with your coffee," I replied amiably.

The pupils of her eyes were huge and black as I took her in my arms.

I stood up in the bathtub, shaving. The general's daughter was fiddling about in the kitchen.

"What news of my father?"

"Not too good," I shouted through the open door. "Your old man gets gloomier every day."

"He's disappointed," she said.

"People always are when things go wrong," I called back.

"What's gone wrong?"

I said: "There's something rotten in the state of Bismarck."

When we had buried the general's diaries in the woods, we sat down on a wall. Below us were the vineyards, and far away the shimmering Rhine. I plucked at the strings of my guitar. *Strong men too have felt the pangs of love,* I hummed.

"Nice, sitting here," said the general's daughter.

"Very nice," said I, "but soon enough the vultures will come for us."

"Ah," she said. "What are you planning to do when it's all over?"

"I'm afraid I haven't the first idea. I never learned a

trade. All I know is how to shout at other people, and shoot them. I've been a soldier all my life."

"It's a very fine profession," she said. "You should make it your career."

"Don't be a fool," said I. "Or do you imagine we Germans are going to be allowed to go on conquering? You must be drunk."

"There are a lot of funny ideas around," she smiled. "Just wait and see."

"Well, I'm off to give Hell the once over."

The general's daughter stood beside the car.

"Look after my father," she said.

I let the engine warm up.

"Bad times are coming," I said, and I slipped into gear.

"The Russians are outside Potsdam and the Yanks have reached Heidelberg."

This was Pigface's greeting to me.

"Let's enjoy what's left of the war," I said with a grin, "because the peace is going to be awful."

We were parked on the edge of the autobahn. The little column containing what remained of the division rolled past. Colonel Olten was traveling at a tremendous clip. His driver pulled up beside us and the colonel wound down his window.

"Bredwitz!" he shouted. "I'll leave a dispatch rider under the roadbridge at the Leipheim clover leaf for you. He'll tell you where to go."

The adjutant nodded, and Olten roared off.

We trundled along behind the battle group. The general lay in the back of the car, wrapped up in a blanket. He was sick, and looked all in.

There was no sign of the dispatch rider.

"Puddinghead saw his chance and hooked it," I remarked to Bredwitz. "He's shoved off, home to mummy."

We drove on to the next village. In the improvised orderly room of the local battle commandant all sorts of soldiers were lying about. There were men from the Luftwaffe, exhausted infantrymen, gunners, tank crews. Two medical orderlies were playing chess. In one corner there was a pile of bazookas and heaven knows what-all in the way of junk.

On the wall hung a placard: COMRADES, EACH STEP BACKWARDS IS DISHONORABLE AND COWARDLY! IT MEANS YOUR DEATH!

An N.C.O. was tapping away at a typewriter.

"Can you rustle me up some gasoline?" asked Bredwitz. "Our car is dry."

"Gasoline?" drawled the N.C.O. without looking up

from his typewriter. "We only issue gasoline against a doctor's prescription."

"Have you gone mad?" roared Bredwitz and crashed his fist down on the table so that pencils and india rubbers sailed through the air.

"And stand up when I'm talking to you," bellowed Bredwitz, in a genuine rage. "Who the devil do you think you are?"

The other soldiers laughed loudly and openly.

"Where is the battle commandant?" snapped Bredwitz.

"With the mayor, sir," replied the N.C.O. He was standing at attention now. His past training was too much for him.

"You, there," he barked at a private. "Take the major to the captain."

As we left the room I looked back.

"The glee club already celebrating the armistice?" I asked.

The soldiers gaped at me.

We hurried through the darkened village. Pale strips of light were occasionally to be seen in the shuttered shop fronts, and from the autobahn came the steady rumble of columns on the move. Driving east. Others headed west. We went along very narrow alleyways and tripped over worn stone steps that led up to a pitch-dark doorway.

"Who's there?" a sulky voice grunted in the darkness.

"Shut up," said the soldier who was acting as our guide. "It's only me."

The man opened the door.

The battle commandant of this one-eyed dump was seated at a table. This captain had an enormous, hydrocephalic head, which suited him. He was stamping documents. On the other side of the table was the mayor, signing them. They looked up, annoyed by our interruption.

The captain growled a greeting. For hours now he and the mayor had been at it, working themselves to a standstill so as to make sure that each and every soldier in his company received a piece of paper stating that its possessor had been formally discharged from the German armed forces. The documents were all dated 1943. It was only a matter of hours before the Americans would arrive, the captain thought nervously, and the discharge papers weren't ready yet. He was haunted by a terrible vision of his men wandering down some main street in Kansas. Nothing but trouble, he thought bitterly.

"Could you tell me where Battlegroup Theodor

Körner is located?" asked Bredwitz. "It must be some-where near here."

The captain scratched his ear. The mayor furrowed his brow.

"Never heard of it," said the captain. "With the best will in the world, I'm afraid I can't be of any help to you whatever. Besides, it's hard to tell one unit from another any more. What I should advise you to do would be to search all the villages systematically, one by one."

"Seems I have no alternative," said Bredwitz. "I wonder if I might ask you for a can of gasoline? Also I shall require a billet for our general. He's sick and I don't really see how I can go on lugging him across country."

The captain groaned.

"A billet for a general? How can I possibly find such a thing? In this village every house is crammed full, to the eaves. We're already taking turns with the beds. A can of gasoline I can willingly let you have, but as for billets I must beg you to try and find something a couple of miles farther south. This morning it might still have been possible, but by noon every bed was gone. We've got an evacuated government department in the village, as well as the remnants of countless staffs. I had the very devil of a time finding beds for them."

What am I supposed to be, a hotel porter? the captain thought to himself.

"Turn somebody out of a bed," said Bredwitz. "The general needs rest and care urgently, and I've got to have the car to find our battle group."

"Kick another gentleman out of bed at this hour of the night?" asked the captain.

His expression was one of astonished incredulity. God help us, he thought. Nothing but trouble, trouble, trouble. And the next time I hear the word battle group I'm going to scream. Every Tom, Dick and Harry is running around in charge of a battle group. A couple of broken-down lorries abandoned by soldiers who've cleared off home, a handful of exhausted stragglers picked up on the highway and hey presto! another battle group. Those gentry can go on fighting their war if they want to. But they can include me out, thought the captain. Me, I've see the red light.

I said to Bredwitz:

"Would the major like me to find a billet for the general?"

"There's no point in your even trying," said the captain. "There's not a single room anywhere in the village with less than three or four men camping in it."

I said: "You'd be surprised how quickly they'll wake up from their lovely dreams if a couple of grenades were suddenly to go bang in the middle of the village street."

I looked as tough as I knew how. The mayor went quite pale when he heard my words.

"We could always see if Farmer Heidl might possibly be able to find a bed for the general," he said.

There you are, God works in a mysterious way, thought I. I'd been in the Army long enough to know that anyhow.

It stank of cow dung. A cold wind whistled down from the mountains. And nothing was the way it used to be. This is home, I thought. But with a bit of luck I might have been born some place else, after all.

The general lay in a peasant's bed. He was feverish and I gave him two pills to take. Whether or not they would do him any good was open to question. But perhaps he would imagine that they did? And that would be something, I thought.

"Horlacher, have you been able to establish exactly where the Americans have got to?" asked the general.

I said: "No, sir. Nothing except the usual rumors. But I can't help feeling they're pretty close now."

"Apart from that, what's happening here?"

"It all seems to be under control, sir. There are tank

blocks everywhere. They've dug foxholes. It looks as though there are plenty of anti-tank guns and machine guns too. But I think it's unlikely the soldiers will put up much of a fight. They're all sick to death of the war."

There was a knock. It was the farmer's wife.

"Do you think that the general would like a glass of warm milk?" she inquired.

"I'm sure he would," said I. If he didn't, I'd drink it.

"Terrible bad luck on the general, all this, isn't it?" whispered the farmer's wife. "Such a good, kind man, too. And now when the Americans arrive he'll lose his job. That's the way life goes, isn't it? Do you think the general might care for a little something to eat?"

"We really don't want to put you to any inconvenience," I said. "But if it's not too much trouble. . . ."

"You're too thoughtful," she whispered excitedly. "If it's not too much trouble. . . ." she said, mimicking me. "Nothing is too much trouble for a German general who has done so much in the service of his country. Oh Jesus, what a misfortune for the poor man! You must pray for him! Only our dear Lord God can help us now. He won't leave us in the lurch!"

And shaking her head, she waddled away toward her kitchen.

"Pleasant people in these parts," said the general.

"Uncommonly obliging," said I.

"Men from this district always make exceptionally good soldiers," announced the general. "They are loyal and have a thoroughly decent point of view. They are patriotic and also well-built. They aren't too bright, it's true, but they make first-class military material."

"There can't be an awful lot of them left, in that case," said I.

"Horlacher, what is the significance of that remark?" snorted the general. "There are plenty of young boys growing up. Just look at the women. They're not the sort of flibbertigibbets who give their children fancy ideas. The mothers here have always been delighted to send their sons off to the Army. A fine, upright soldier is the pride and joy of the family in these parts."

"They're also very religious," I said.

"Which is extremely important," announced the general. "It results in a decent family life, and guarantees the children a proper education in which they'll be taught to respect the State as they should. You wait and see the magnificent recruits this district will provide in ten or fifteen years' time. They'll be something to make a new start with!"

As dawn was breaking there came the clatter and rattle of tank tracks from the autobahn.

Small cross-country vehicles twisted past the anti-tank obstacles. Machine guns rat-a-tatted. Cannons roared and shells whistled through the mist. The Americans had arrived.

I saw them arrive. They were walking along a narrow path across a field. In front stalked a man with a Tommy gun, and the face of a homicidal maniac. Behind him came a file of faithful G.I.s. One man had stopped for a pee.

I stood at the window and gawked. A cow mooed in its stall. So this is it, I thought. I heard the latch open. What sort of hoops are these bastards going to put us through? Funny sort of hangover. Should I shout something at them about how the German military machine had deprived me of my childhood beliefs?

What should I do?

The one with the Tommy gun was the first to enter the room. He stank of cognac. He moved in a cloud of brandy. And the muzzle of his Tommy gun was pointed at my navel.

"Hello, Kraut," he grunted.

"Morning, Jack," said I.

"Wise guy, eh? Been in it a long time, eh? Seventh Kraut Army, I bet?" he asked with a wink.

"That's right," said I.

He noticed the general's uniform jacket, gave a low whistle, and glanced at the bed.

"It's a general," he said, "and you're one of the guys that struck it good."

The one with the Tommy gun looked as happy as a hangman with a job to do.

THE general lay on a narrow bed, in a prison cell. He no longer possessed anything, or was anybody. He wore an old pair of pajamas and, as always, woolen socks. For the past few days they had allowed me to look after him again.

I brought him his breakfast.

"Good morning, sir."

"God be with you, my friend."

I placed the tray upon the bed and poured tea into the cup.

"Can't that fellow leave me alone even for five minutes?" asked the general.

He was annoyed by the sergeant who stood in the passage outside the open door of the cell, where he could watch every gesture the general made.

"That cow-face of his gets on my nerves," whispered the general. "He even watches me when I use the can. Every mouthful I swallow, every time I take a sip of water, he's watching. I can't move a muscle without him gawking at me."

"I'm sure he doesn't do it on purpose," I said. "I mean, he's had his orders, and he's simply carrying them out."

"No doubt they've also told him to pay particular attention every time I fart," growled the general.

He swallowed a little tea.

"Did you sleep well, sir?" I asked.

"Wonderfully!" he boomed. "If they'd hung a noose around my neck last night I'd never have noticed it."

"They won't do that," I said.

"And why not, my friend? That's what they've brought me here for. Do you imagine they want to hear my views on the relative advantages and disadvantages of socks for the infantry? Hey, Sergeant," he called out, "what are you planning to do with me?"

The sergeant did not understand. He took a step forward into the cell.

"Doctor? You want doctor?" he asked in pidgin German.

"What sort of a doctor?" rumbled the general. "A couple of yards of rope is pretty good medicine too, isn't it? It'll cure most illnesses."

Christ on a bicycle, I thought angrily, why the hell must he talk like that? He'll simply destroy any goodwill they might otherwise have for him.

"You shouldn't bait the sergeant like that, sir," I advised him.

The general leaned back. He just managed to replace the teacup on the tray. His hands still gripped it, unable to let it go. His body was shaken by waves of pain.

"What the devil can it be?" he murmured. "I feel so well, otherwise."

But he was a sick man. He lay in the prison cell and

drew deep breaths of stale air. He forced himself to smile.

"Is it better now?" I asked.

"I've got a terrible pain in my stomach," he whispered. I was sitting on the stool beside the bed.

I looked at him closely. He was lying perfectly still, his eyes fixed on the ceiling. After a little while his expression showed a trace of the old defiance once again.

God damn it, what a filthy business, I thought. Why do they have to put him in a prison of all places?

The M.P. lieutenant came into the cell.

"Hello, sir," he said with a grin.

He was a strapping great fellow. At the time of the Normandy landing he'd succeeded in laying his hands on eleven million francs, which he had successfully changed into dollars. He grinned all the time.

"Everything O.K.?" he asked. "Anything I can do for you?"

"Nothing, thank you," said the general.

"If you do need anything, just ask the sergeant here," said the lieutenant.

He walked out, and we heard him say to the sentry in the corridor:

"Better reserve a table in Valhalla for that old Teuton." His tone was sarcastic.

"That an officers' club for Krauts?" snickered the sergeant.

"Horlacher, did you hear what they said?" the general whispered angrily.

I said: "Yes, sir, but there's nothing whatever we can do about it. Don't let it get you down, sir."

"One day there'll be marble plaques put up on the walls of this prison," growled the general.

The doctor came.

"Well?" he asked. He snatched the general's hand and felt his pulse.

"Temperature's up a bit," he stated.

The doctor dropped some tablets into a glass of water which he then handed to the general.

"Why don't you have him moved to the hospital?" I asked the doctor.

"Not possible," he said.

"In any civilized country a man in his condition would be taken to a hospital," I said.

"It would have been a good thing if your compatriots had remembered to behave in so humane a fashion," said the doctor. He took the glass from the general and placed it on one side.

After which all was quiet in the cell. Even when the doctor had gone we said nothing for a time.

"What did the fool mean by that remark of his?" I asked. Though I knew exactly what the doctor had meant. "What concern is it of his, the political corpses in the German concentration camps?"

The general sighed.

"Horlacher," he said. "You musn't take these people too seriously. They've won a war and so now they imagine they must put on this holier-than-thou act with us."

"Why, though, should that sawbones spit out his hatred in this cell of all places? It's revolting," I said. "How about honor among soldiers?"

Why in God's name did the man have to talk such drivel? I thought. Weren't we deep enough in it, already? Do they have to piss on us as well? Then I thought: for Christ's sake what a waste of nervous energy, worrying about a thing like that.

"They want to see us Germans walking about in sackcloth and ashes," said the general. "What a hope! Incidentally, I wouldn't mind a drink. Do you think you could manage to rustle me up something?"

"Certainly, sir," said I.

I was the general's soldier-servant. What he said, went. That was my life.

As I left the cell the loudspeakers were summoning a sentry to the guardroom. For some reason or other this announcement was followed by noisy dance music. It started with a simple cowboy song, played so loudly that I jumped.

The sergeant, whose job it was to watch the general, was sashaying about in time to the music.

I said: "Jack, buy me a bottle of hooch, will you? My old man really needs a drop of something."

"Goddammit, that old squarehead wants a drink now, does he? As far as I'm concerned, you can pour hydrochloric acid down his throat," he said nastily. "Hell, I'll be glad to see the last of him."

"You'd really like it if they hanged him?"

"It's not for me to hold up a Christian when he's headed for the pearly gates," grinned the sergeant.

I said: "If you feel any strong personal desire to hear the celestial choir, just lend me that gun of yours for five seconds, and I'll make you a present of a first-class ticket to paradise, free, gratis and for nothing."

"You're a funny one," laughed the sergeant. "A proper shit-kraut."

He leaned against the wall and yawned.

"God, this is a boring job," he said.

"Come on, how about the hooch?" I asked.

"Go and see Gregory, he'll give you one."

"You're a good guy," I said.

"And I reckon the information is worth one dollar."

"I'm the kindest man you ever saw and I'm gentle as a lamb," Gregory informed me. "But I'm not selling you a bottle of anything. If you want a drink, O.K., help yourself. But not for your old man. Why, I wouldn't even give him a glass of spit. Because I'm a Jew, you see. A yid, an Ikey! The goddamned murder club, to which your old man belonged, bumped off my entire family in Warsaw."

"I know all about what happened in Warsaw," I said. "But my old man had absolutely nothing whatever to do with it."

"That's what you say. Isn't he sitting here because he had Maquis people shot?"

"Listen, man, they were Communists," I explained.

"Put another record on. I'm tired of that one," Gregory yawned.

"As far as I'm concerned," I said, "you can take your booze and stuff it. And I hope it gives you piles."

It wasn't that I hadn't understood the mess waiter's point of view. I just didn't happen to like his tone. Couldn't he present his arguments a little more politely?

On the first floor I ran into the M.P. lieutenant.

"What are you doing wandering about up here?" he asked me sharply. "You know you're not allowed in this part of the building. If the boss catches you, you'll be in for it."

I told him what I was after.

"You're wasting your time with those boys," he said. "They'll do nothing for you."

"They treated us with a bit more respect when the fighting was on," I said.

"Come with me," said the lieutenant. "I'll give you a bottle from my private store. And if the boss catches you with it, tell him it was a present from the Salvation Army."

"They drink pretty good in that army, don't they?" I said as I followed him down the corridor.

"Your old man's one of the meanest bastards I ever saw," announced the lieutenant. "All the same, I can't help liking him, because he's the real McCoy all right. No half-measures about him, the genuine jack-booted bastard. I guess they'd have made him a general in my country too."

"I can well believe you," said I.

I poured out a little brandy and passed the general the glass. His hands trembled.

"I'll only drink enough to stop the pain," he said. "Just the absolute minimum."

I felt I could do with a drink myself, and I looked around for another glass.

Colonel Kaye walked in through the open door. He saw the bottle but ignored it.

"Sir, would you do me a favor?" he asked the general, thrusting a large photograph under the old man's nose. "Would you be so good as to sign this? We'd like to hang it up in our club back home."

"Why not take our skulls across the Atlantic as souvenirs?" grunted the general. "And turn them into beer steins, with a tin lid and a built-in musical box. Whenever you took a swallow they'd play you a genuine Prussian march."

The colonel gave a loud laugh.

"Wonderful ideas you have," he said. "Only our people back home wouldn't see the point."

"I know all about your people," said the general. "Terribly thorough, isn't that right? I bet there's someone busy at this moment sterilizing the rope you're going to hang me with."

"Why do you keep on talking about being hanged?" asked the colonel. "How many times must I tell you that there's absolutely no question of your being condemned to death? You'll simply be handed over to the French. That's all that will happen to you."

"Really?" said the general, and he squinted up at the colonel. "Give me the photo," he said. I watched him while he signed it.

Big, clear letters.

"Now I've got all the signatures," said the colonel with evident joy. "All the big shots. I'd like to have had your Supreme Commander's too, but that wasn't possible, unfortunately."

"Must be a great disappointment to you," said the general.

"I don't believe they poured gasoline over his corpse in Berlin and burned it. Or else why should he have said he wanted to be buried in the Warriors' Memorial at Munich? That corpse-burning act was just another of his tricks, if you ask me. With a couple of charred bones and a button or two you can't prove anything. I think they walled him up somewhere or other. Like Siegfried and all that stuff. I'm quite certain one day somebody will find the skeleton and make a national holy relic out of it."

"I wish I had your worries," smiled the general. "All the same, you're a good psychologist. You seem to understand us."

"You know, sir," said the talkative colonel, "you Germans make it terribly easy for us. It's so simple to see through your tricks. Because they're always the same, regardless of circumstances. It seems to me that the Germans who write your history and practice your politics spend their time sitting on a merry-go-round. Sometimes it goes slow, sometimes it goes fast, but it's always the same old carousel."

"Once you're on board you can't jump off," said the general. "Or you'll land flat on your face."

"True enough," remarked the colonel.

Why does my general wear socks in bed? I wondered. Is it low blood pressure that makes his feet cold?

"Tomorrow I hand over to my replacement," announced the prison commandant. "I hope you haven't any complaints to make about your treatment here under me?"

"None whatever," the general assured him. "You can go home to your family with a clear conscience."

"I've got no family," said the Colonel. "I'm all alone. Once I'm back in the States I'm going to pack my bags and go into a Spanish monastery, a Trappist one."

"Most extraordinary!" said the general. "Do you really feel cut out for that sort of life?"

"I think so," said the colonel. "Do you know Spain?"

"I've never been beyond San Sebastian," said the general. "But I can imagine what the country is like."

"I'd rather be going to Greece," said the colonel. "But it seems it's not possible. Do you know Greece?"

"Athens. And so on," said the general.

"Extraordinarily interesting country, Greece."

"Yes, very."

After a little while the colonel said good-bye.

"I'll step in again before I leave," he said in his soft and sibilant voice.

He smiled and nodded.

"Horlacher, did you hear what he said? They're planning to send me to France."

"Yes, sir, I heard."

"Fate plays some queer tricks on us," murmured the general.

I could see that he was thinking about his travels in France in years gone by. With a revolver in his pocket instead of a passport.

The general's daughter had booked a room in a small hotel not far from the prison. At midday I went to see her.

"Have you got your visitor's permit yet?" I asked.

"It'll be ready in two or three hours."

I said: "You'd better reckon on four or six hours. You're dealing with the military, you know."

The waiter came.

"Can you bring us a drink?" I asked.

"Only if you pay in dollars."

"I guessed from your face you weren't interested in German money."

He gave a sour smile.

"Where did you get your dollars from?" asked the general's daughter.

"I sold my medals," I said.

We sat there, avoiding one another's eyes. Over the washbasin hung a notice: PLEASE DO NOT THROW

PAPER TOWELS OR RAZOR BLADES IN HERE. Then the waiter brought us a bottle and two glasses.

"Do you want cigarettes?" he asked.

I said: "I can sell them to you."

"How much?"

"Five dollars a carton."

"I'll buy as many as you've got at that price."

"All right," I said. "See you this evening."

"How do you get hold of cigarettes?" the general's daughter wanted to know.

"Easy," I said. "These boys would sell you a battleship or a tank if you wanted one."

"Fantastic," she said.

"They're not like us."

"Now I want a kiss," I said.

"That's fatal with us," she smiled.

She got up and closed the door.

"Come here," I said.

"What have you done to me?" she whispered.

"Me to you?"

While she undressed I looked at her legs. I folded my trousers and hung them over the back of a chair. A man and a woman were walking along the corridor, past the door. They were laughing together.

In the next room somebody was brushing his teeth.

"Look at me a bit more like that," she whispered.

She's got wonderful green eyes, I thought.

"I like it when you look at me that way."

"Not so loud," I whispered in her ear.

"I could yell."

"We've got it bad, both of us," I said.

We went downstairs and sat in the dining room. I asked the waiter for coffee. "The real stuff that does you good."

"Pay in dollars then?" he said.

The man was a positive hyena.

"How long will I have to sit around here and wait?" asked the general's daughter.

She took out her lipstick and began to paint her lips.

I said: "At least four to six hours. You must reckon on that."

She looked at her watch.

At the next table was seated a bald-headed, overfed old booby wearing what looked like shooting clothes made out of a remodeled uniform. He was guzzling tea. He stared at us and then got up and came across to our table.

"Did I hear you say you're waiting for a visitor's permit?" he asked.

"So what?" said I.

"Well, I'm waiting for one too."

"So what?" said I.

He fluttered his eyelids and looked pie-faced.

"Forgive me, please, forcing my company on you like this," he said. "But it's really awful. I've been waiting for weeks now for a visitor's permit. I simply don't get anywhere with them. The waiter told me you are expecting to get your permit today. Have you any contacts which might be of help to me?"

He raised his head and licked his lips. He was staring at the general's daughter, his eyes wide open.

"We have no special contacts," I said.

He rolled his eyes miserably toward the ceiling.

"I'd thought you'd be able to help me," he whispered. "I've been waiting for weeks."

"Take a powder," I said.

"Let him be," said the general's daughter.

"Does his whining amuse you?" I asked.

"Oh God, oh God, if I could only just see him once," groaned Fatty. "Just once, so that he knows I'm here and waiting for him. Is it not quite dreadful to have been so respected in the old days, and now to be reduced to this? Have you actually seen the cells? Are they really just like the cells in an ordinary prison? And what about the guards? What sort of guards do they have?"

"Don't worry," I said. "The guards won't rape your sweetheart."

Tears began to trickle down his cheeks.

"I wonder if you can understand? We've known each other ever since we were tiny children, and we've always been together. I've never cared anything about politics. If I'd known at the time that this was going to happen I'd never have let him get mixed up with those people at all. I give you my word of honor he never made the slightest effort to advance his career. It was all his family's fault, do you understand? They wanted it that way. His father was a senior civil servant."

"Take a powder," I said.

"Please accept my apologies a hundred times. It wasn't my intention to butt in. Quite the contrary. I only thought you might be able to help me because the waiter said you're getting a visitor's permit today."

"Buzz off," I said.

He bowed and backed away from our table. His eyes were the color of forget-me-nots.

"Why were you so nasty to him?" asked the general's daughter.

"I've got my own worries."

"Do you never think about anything except yourself? I, I, I."

"Charity begins at home," said I. "Or else you can become a captain in the Salvation Army."

Damn it, I thought. Why must she talk to me in that tone of voice?

"You always avoid any sort of serious conversation. Why? Is it because you're too stupid?"

I said: "The chief thing is to keep physically fit. Then understanding grows on its own. At least that's what they told me when I was a recruit at the depot."

The waiter brought us our coffee.

"Was he annoying you?" he asked, nodding toward Fatty at the next table.

"Not in the slightest," said the general's daughter.

"I can tell you, I'm sick to death of him," the waiter said. "He's got a friend in the prison over there. But visitor's permits are only issued to wives and children. Which in this particular case is a lot of nonsense, if you understand what I mean."

"No, I don't," said I. "Tell us more, it's fascinating."

"Please leave us alone," said the general's daughter.

"Why did you send him away?" I asked. "That had the makings of a highly serious conversation. Topical, too."

"Must you always work off your bad temper on other people?"

"Why not? That's the way I am."

"It's about time you pulled yourself together."

"A new age has begun."

A door slammed on the first floor. A man came

down the stairs. Behind him, on very high heels, there tripped an overdressed doll.

"Darling, don't run so," she wailed.

The man threw a banknote on the bar. The waiter gave him three packets of cigarettes for it. The girl stood there, twisting her neck to examine a ladder in her stocking. A minute later they'd both gone.

"This waiting about is frightful," said the general's daughter.

She fiddled with her coffee spoon.

"If nothing happens within the next half-hour," I said, "I'll go across and ask the security officer what the hell has happened to your pass."

Behind the bar the waiter was polishing glasses. The fat man sat at his table, watching a fly cleaning its wings.

"Do you want another coffee?" I asked.

"It's too expensive," said the general's daughter.

I said: "True enough. Prices here are criminal. How about a game of billiards?"

She looked about her.

"The billiards table's in the next room," I said. "I noticed it earlier."

"Do you want something?" the waiter asked.

He had muddy eyes, like a sewer rat.

"You have a billiards table next door, haven't you?" I asked.

"Yes," he said. "Would you like a game? There's no charge."

"That's handsome," I said.

The door opened and the M.P. lieutenant walked in.

"Hullo!" he said with a smile. "I thought I'd find you here."

I said to the general's daughter:

"This is one of the guards. Very decent fellow. He's the one who gave me the bottle for the general."

"I'm pleased to meet you," she said.

"This is the general's daughter," I explained to the lieutenant.

He examined her the way a cow examines a new manger.

"Unfortunately you won't be able to visit your father before this evening," he said.

"Why's that?" I asked. "Something special going on?"

"No," said the lieutenant and smiled, "just a whim of the security officer's. He was born a German, you know, and he gets a hell of a kick out of annoying his fellow-countrymen."

"Do you want something to drink?" the waiter asked the lieutenant.

"No," he said. "I'm going to the club. Being on duty over there gives me the willies. I need a bit of a break now and then."

"I can believe you," I said.

"Would you like to come along for a while? You've only got to wear my raincoat and no one will know you're a German," he said. "I'm sure you'd enjoy it," he added to the general's daughter, and gave her a beaming smile.

"Is that done these days?" she asked.

I said: "A change won't do us any harm either."

"Wonderful the way you can switch your moods," she said.

At the club a grinning G.I. was celebrating the day his mother nearly died. "Happy birthday to you . . ." they bawled in chorus.

The club was overheated. It stank like a hairdresser's.

The lieutenant ordered whisky and hamburgers.

"Excuse me," he then said, "I've got a bit of business to see to."

I said: *"Sieg heil* and happy looting."

We sat alone at the table and I tried to show what good manners I had. There were girls all around us, gabbling away nineteen to the dozen. On the stage another girl was crooning. She wore a dress which would have sent any horrified German public prosecutor thumbing feverishly through the penal code. She sang, rather badly, in a nasal voice: *I wish I had a paper doll to call my own. . . .*

She pretended that the mike was her imaginary dolly. Then she jigged about a bit and sang another song about the big bad wolf and the seven little deers. Six of the deers let the wolf eat them, but not the seventh. When he came to that one, the big bad wolf got a nasty shock, because the seventh deer was the singer herself. She pulled a revolver from under her dress and fired half a dozen blank cartridges at the wolf, wham, wham, wham. You see, the wolf didn't know that this particular deer had seen long service with the U.S. Seventh Army and had therefore learned how to deal with creatures such as him.

What next? I thought.

The general's daughter was deciphering a notice posted by the door.

GIRLS ARE FORBIDDEN TO SIT ON THEIR SWEET-HEARTS' LAPS EXCEPT WITH A CUSHION IN BETWEEN. That was what it said.

The lieutenant reappeared.

"Fun here, isn't it?" he asked and gazed about him with a satisfied expression.

I said: "Whom God will truly favor show, him sends He out into the world."

"Where've you been all afternoon?" the sergeant in

the corridor outside the cell asked me.

"Been taking part in a sack-race for the over-forties," I said.

"You're an uppity bastard," grunted the sergeant. "You Krauts are an uppity crowd altogether. But when you're treated a bit tough it's another story. I've seen it and I know. Back at the command post we had a tent with a Counter Intelligence Corps captain in it, interrogating captured Krauts. The P.O.W.s were lined up on this side of the tent, and went in one by one. After a while they came out at the other end of the tent, which was where I was. I had a Colt and each time one of them came out I fired a couple of shots in the air. Inside the tent the captain would be interrogating the next Kraut. He'd say, well, son, what about you, are you another of these tough guys who won't talk? You should have seen it. They soon stopped acting uppity. Every damn one of them talked, without exception."

"Filthy trick," I said.

"Perfectly legal," said the sergeant. "Who's to say I can't fire my revolver in the air if I want to?"

"Extraordinary how you get such ideas," I said. "But I suppose nothing's surprising in a country where the men have to do the housework and Hollywood harlots set the social tone."

"There's still a couple of empty cells on the third

floor," grinned the sergeant. "If you want to see the inside of one of them, just go right on talking."

I looked up. Guards were leaning against the railings that separated the corridor from the central hall. The sergeant fished a handkerchief out of his pocket and blew his nose. His trumpeting re-echoed unpleasantly throughout the building.

The prison cat came strolling along the corridor.

I said: *"Miez! Miez!"*

The sergeant said:

"She's an American cat. She don't know what that means."

"So I notice," said I.

I walked over to the barred window and stared out at the streets. There were M.P.s lolling about. And kids waiting for one of them to throw away a cigarette butt. I saw shabbily dressed people.

Inside the building someone flushed a toilet.

THEY had handed the general over to the French. They gave me a piece of paper which said I'd been released from P.O.W. camp.

"Scram off home," they said.

Home, that's a good one, I thought. I went to the general's daughter.

"What's going to happen now?" she asked. "We can't live on love alone. How are we going to keep our heads above water?"

"Needs some concentrated thought," said I.

"We'll have to make money somehow or other. Enough to ensure a decent life for my father when he comes home eventually."

I said: "You're dead right. But what shall we do?"

The general's daughter walked up and down. She frowned. She stared at her fingernails.

"We mustn't lose heart," she said. "That's the principal thing. You know the story about the two frogs who fell into the pail of milk?"

"I do," said I. "One frog drowned. The other went on struggling till he'd made a piece of butter to sit on."

"That's what we've got to do."

"It's going to be a regular catch-as-catch-can," I said. "And for why? Because all those clever politicians have mucked us up good and proper. When we were

kids at school they started in on their brain-washing,
telling us what grand fellows they were and how they
were only there to serve the people. Gave themselves
nervous breakdowns worrying about us, they said, and
they grew fat on it. While at home my old man was
pinning my ears back with stories about the joys of
Army life. Because he wanted to be rid of me, the old
twister. And believe it or not, I fell for it. Real keen,
I was, for a military career. My schoolteachers said
it was just the life for me, too. So off I go, faithful unto
death and all the rest of it. The nation's shield and
bulwark, that's what we were, the guardians of peace
and freedom. Next thing you know there's a war on.
And nowadays nobody ever wanted it. Tut, tut! they
say, and they press a special watch into the blind men's
hands which tells them whether the sun's shining or
the moon. A man who's had a bullet through his head
gets a nice bit of stainless steel to keep his brains dry
when it's raining. And for us old soldiers, a small tip
because we didn't fill our pants when the guns went
off. . . ."

"Oh shut up," said the general's daughter. "Or do
you want to send yourself round the bend?"

She woke me up with a sharp jab in the ribs.
"Wake up!" she said loudly. "Will you wake up!"
Her voice was quite shrill, and she pulled my hair.

"What's the matter? It's still pitch dark."

She was jigging about in the bed.

"I've got it," she said, softly now. "Shall I tell you what we'll do? We're going to make schnapps. We've got masses of fruit. I can find the sugar, and we'll get our fuel from the woods."

"And five years in the lock-up from the public prosecutor," I said.

"Oh, you're so stupid," she said.

"Think it over," said I. "And first of all work out where you're going to organize your distillery gear from. And me, I'd like to go on sleeping."

"We've got an old wood-burning boiler down in the cellar. Couldn't we fix that up?" she asked.

"You've got the most wonderful ideas, duckums," said I. "Do we really want to blow ourselves up with a schnapps machine? Honestly, I ask you, give your mind a rest. Good night."

"I know how to make schnapps. Grandpa's peasants showed me."

"Just proves what lousy pay you gave your people," I said. "Not even enough for the poor bastards to buy a decent bottle of booze."

"Will you stop talking such nonsense," she hissed. "What do you know about that sort of thing? If you pay them a penny more than they need, what do they do with the money? Spend it on a lot of rubbishy trash they're better off without. You're a fool to talk about it, because you know nothing. Try and think how we can fix up a distillery instead."

Months passed. At last the distillery was rigged up and drops of drinkable liquor began to trickle down its twisted pipes.

I'd discovered a refugee who knew how to fix machinery. His name was Rentzsch, and he was a decent fellow. He built us a still in the old wash-house, and it worked. In exchange he was to get 10 per cent of the profits. This was a lot of dough for him. Enough to feed his family on. And our livelihood was dead certain. Not a particularly respectable career, but a reliable one.

I'd written Pigface a letter. One day I saw his plumpudding head grinning at me over the garden fence. "Remember when we didn't have to work to eat? Those were the days."

"You don't look exactly undernourished," I said.

"How much do you clear on the bottle?" he asked with obvious curiosity. "The schnapps business ticking over all right?"

"Do you think I asked you here because of your pretty face?"

Pigface laughed.

"Polite as ever," he said. "Seriously, though, I can't afford any pleasure trips around the country just now. I can only get away if there's a good chance of making something out of it. There's all sorts of things cooking at the moment. Though you wouldn't notice it here in the Black Forest. All you see here is the Frogs carting our wood away. Talking about carting things away, what news of our old man?"

"No idea," said I. "Damn it all, I'll never understand why a German general should have to sit in the lock-up simply because he ordered a few Communists shot. Where's the justice in it?"

"When people start squawking about justice it always means they've landed in the cart," said Pigface with a grin.

"Sad but true," said I. "Well, come on into the parlor and we'll talk business, you old goldbrick."

We sent our home-made booze to Hamburg in bottles labeled vinegar. Pigface paid in coconut fat, which we swapped for margarine from a margarine factory. The margarine we exchanged for American cigarettes, or anything else that was handy.

Olten wrote to the general's daughter as soon as he was discharged from his P.O.W. camp. The general's misfortunes troubled him deeply, he said. He had to write and tell her how upset he was about it, he said. Otherwise, all best wishes, likewise from his wife.

Armed with the food parcel, I went to see him. Olten was living among ruins. A slut opened the door.

"Next time you want to see that old warmonger, ring three times," she snarled at me.

"My apologies, Madame," I said. "I trust you weren't sitting on the can?"

She grunted and grumbled, then shouted down the hall: "Somebody at the door!"

She vanished. Doors banged. I waited.

A fancy-looking youth wearing very short shorts came skidding down the stairs. He ogled me. There was the noise of felt slippers shuffling along the corridor. Olten stood before me. He did not give me time to say hello, but grabbed my arm and hurried me across the hall, which was crammed with trunks, boxes and packing cases. I bumped into an open door.

"Here we are!" said Olten, opened the door a little wider, and pushed me into an untidy room.

It was crowded with furniture. The colonel's wife was seated in an old-fashioned armchair, a robe over her knees. On a table stood three photographs, two young men and a girl even younger. Beside them lay

Iron Crosses and Assault Badges, and the photograph frames were covered with black crêpe.

Three corpses in one family is a bit steep, I thought. Even the finest fatherland is hardly worth that.

I said: "How do you do, Mrs. Olten? The general's daughter asked me to pay you her respects."

"Is the parcel for us?" asked Olten.

"Yes, Colonel," I said.

"Don't say colonel so loudly," whispered Olten nervously. "They've filled our house with the most dreadful people. They make our life hell. The whole gang hate soldiers, and they don't try to hide it. It's a horrible business," he sighed. "I was well aware that things would be difficult, but I never imagined it could be as bad as this."

"This time they're giving us the works," I said.

"Yesterday my old coalman stopped me in the street," Olten related. "Do you know what he wanted? He said I could help him deliver the coal!"

"They've got some queer ideas nowadays, those people," I said.

"Day before yesterday I went to the labor exchange. There was a scruffy-looking fellow seated behind the desk. The sort of man I'd have given seven days to, for not getting his hair cut, in the Army. He grinned at me and said the only jobs available at the moment were cleaning the streets!"

"We ought to make a note of the names of jerks like that," I said. "So as one day we can give them a good spanking for their cheek and impudence."

"Do you really mean that?"

"I do indeed," said I.

"I wish I were as ingenuous as you," said Olten.

He fished an aged pipe from his pocket and began to clean it thoroughly, scraping at the burned wood with a small penknife.

"You see the world through rose-tinted spectacles," he said. "Those times will never come again. The German nation will be turned into a race of gardeners."

"The general's daughter doesn't agree with you at all about that," I said. "She thinks it's entirely up to us if we want to have an army again."

"The problem isn't as simple as that," said Olten. "The victor nations have got the last word, you know. We must never forget that."

I said: "The general's daughter believes it's simply a question of playing our cards properly, politically that is. If we can make the proposition appear attractive enough, they'll swallow it."

"Horlacher, you keep referring to the general's daughter. Do you see her frequently?"

"I do indeed," I said. "I'm living in her house. The way I look at it is this. The general saved my life in the war, by making me his driver. Therefore, to show my gratitude, I'm doing what I can to help the general's daughter over a difficult patch. I give her a hand in the house and garden. When the general comes home, he'll need me again. That's certain. So I'll wait there till he does."

Olten gazed at me with amazement.

"What do you think of that?" he said to his wife.

She said nothing, and smiled at the wall before her. Off her rocker, I said to myself.

"In an age of utter decadence a simple soldier preserves his loyalty to his old commander, while officers are running around fighting for the honor of polishing their conquerors' boots," said Olten.

He shook his head.

"And funnily enough I was always convinced in the old days that you were a peculiarly obnoxious fellow," he said, looking me straight in the face.

I said: "We all make mistakes from time to time."

"They're both up the creek," I informed the general's daughter. "They're in it to here," I explained. "Nothing to look forward to, nothing to look back on, not a penny in their pockets. The room they live in is a pigsty. He's got no job and she sits in front of the pictures of her kids and weeps."

"I knew them. They were fine children," said the general's daughter. "One fell in France, the other in

Norway. The daughter was a hospital nurse, killed in the bombing."

"A war like that is a damned expensive joke for some families," I said. "There's not everyone can afford three corpses at one go."

Rentzsch was a thin man and almost bald. He was a nervous chain-smoker, with permanently yellow fingers.

"I hope nobody discovers what we're doing here," he said, as he controlled the pressure in the still. "I never would have believed I'd be reduced to this," he moaned to himself.

"Rentzsch, stop whining," I said. "To hear you talk anyone would think we were turning little girls into sausage meat. What's so wicked in what we're doing? We're thumbing our nose at a State monopoly, that's all."

"It's against the law," Rentzsch whispered timidly.

"Don't make me laugh," I said. "Now that you've got something in your belly and clean socks on your feet, your conscience is beginning to act up. Is that it? I can remember when you'd have gone through fire and water to get this distillery going."

"Necessity knows no laws!" said Rentzsch. "Believe me, if I hadn't had a family to support I would never have let myself become involved in such a business.

Why, I'd rather have worked day and night, I'd rather
sweat blood, than distil illegal alcohol."

"It's all a matter of taste, as the dog said when he
licked the cat's behind," I laughed. I was sitting at an
old kitchen table, sticking labels that said VINEGAR on
to the bottles of schnapps.

The wash-house smelt of rotten vegetables. Glowing
wood sparks fell from the fire under the boiler, hissed
on the damp concrete, and turned black. The cellar
windows were blacked out, and shut fast.

"We are sinning against the laws of our country,"
said Rentzsch.

"Maybe one day your country will remit your taxes
in gratitude for your high principles," said I.

Rentzsch threw down a piece of wood he was holding.

"I'm going to quit soon. I might as well do so right
away," he said.

"Suits me," said I. "We can keep the business going
without your help."

What a drip, I thought.

"I can understand a man not wanting to chance his
arm," I said to him. "But what sort of a job do you
think you'll get in times like these? With your training
and background you won't find no red carpets laid out
for you."

"I've got a plan, and I think it's a pretty good one."

Rentzsch came across to the table and watched me sticking on the labels.

"There's a bombed-out machine-tool factory near Esslingen, where they used to make die stamps," he said. "The owner is looking for an expert who's capable of getting it going again."

"You mean he's looking for a mug?" I said. "Rentzsch, are you an engineer or are you a scrap peddler? My advice to you, cobbler, is stick to your last. We'll make a few more gallons of schnapps together until some better job turns up for you. That way you'll be paid in cash and your kids won't go hungry."

"Horlacher, I'm telling you, this factory could be made into something!" Rentzsch insisted. "The concrete roof is down; but the machines are buried underneath it. They'll be rusty all right, still they can be put in working order again. It's insane not to use such valuable equipment. We'll have to work all right! Roll up our sleeves and get on with the job! For me that would be a wonderful life, doing something constructive, having an object in life again!"

His sunken eyes were fixed on mine, questioning.

"You need a lot of money to start up a factory," he said.

"What about it?" said I.

"He's a maniac," I told the general's daughter. "The sort that's crazy for work. When he talks about his heap of rubble you'd think it was the famous donkey that used to drop gold. On the other hand, this story of his about the machine-tool factory might be the finger of God."

The general's daughter grinned.

"I'll get to the bottom of it."

I was working in the garden. There was plenty to do. Digging, for instance; and phosphates for the fruit trees; and pulling up the weeds. I was wondering about the tomatoes—maybe it'd be a good idea to train them at an angle this year—when the general's daughter appeared.

She looked around. "Wonderful the way you've tidied it all up," she said.

"I want your old man to be pleased, when he comes home," I said.

"He always thought a lot of his garden," said she, and broke off a couple of dead leaves.

I went on working. The general's daughter watched me.

"I've got hold of a German lawyer and a French one," she told me. "First-class men. And they're quite sure they can arrange for my father to be sent home."

The general's daughter had had an exhausting trip. She'd been away for over a week.

"What's it like out there?" I asked.

"Terrible. Misery and wretchedness everywhere. Most Germans are dressed in rags, and lots are starving. Everything's bombed flat. Rubble and ashes, that's all."

She sat down wearily on a bench.

"I went over the machine-tool factory Rentzsch told you about," she said.

I stuck my spade into the ground and looked at her eagerly.

"I even persuaded the proprietor to let me go halves with him. Rentzsch is to be chief engineer. So he'll have a good job and a regular salary, which is worth having after all."

"I'd like to see Rentzsch's face when you tell him. Incidentally, where's the money coming from?"

"Have you ever worked out how much we make out of our booze?" she said with a smile. "At least fifty thousand per hundred bottles. Or a hundred cartons. The current value of one cigarette is seven marks."

"I can't work it out in my head," I said. "I'll go and fetch a piece of paper and a pencil."

"Don't bother. Leave it to me."

Jumping Jesus, I thought, how much does that make? And in the Army I often hadn't got enough brass to wet my whistle.

"If that's the way it goes, let's start another distillery quick," I said.

"And have even more smoke pouring out of the chimneys?" the general's daughter replied. She was clearly against this idea. "No, we'd better watch out. We've gone as far as we dare. It's dangerous."

"No more dangerous than life in the Army, running around with live grenades in your trouser pockets," I said.

"Not a very apt comparison," sighed the general's daughter. "You've no idea how complicated civilian life actually is. It was all much easier in the Army. We were big shots then."

"That's right," said I. "Why, they even had to salute us in those days! And what do those jerks do now? Hurry past us with their noses in the air."

"But not for very much longer," prophesied the general's daughter.

I said: "I hope to God you're right."

Rentzsch needed masses of money. Also he couldn't get on without steel girders. Then a compressor was really essential, after which he was yelling for tiles and cement. He wanted wood and tarpaper and nails and tools and stapling machines and signatures and grub for the workmen.

The general's daughter was bad tempered and exhausted.

"I'm fed up," she said loudly and plunked herself down in an armchair. "Absolutely fed up. Fed to the teeth."

"We took on something with that Rentzsch," said I. "He's the sort of man who can do anything provided he's got everything he needs for the job. If he hasn't, he just stands there like a cow in a thunderstorm. He'll have us all climbing up the wall before he's through."

"Is that all you can think to say, you dumb ox?" she shouted at me. "Haven't you got any ideas at all in that thick head of yours? Can't you do anything except sneer at a man who's working while you water the cacti and smoke fat cigars?"

"And who scrubs out the toilet and makes the schnapps?"

"For every bag of cement and every gross of nails I've got to argue and bargain till I'm hoarse." The general's daughter was all set for a good long squawk. "I sleep in buggy hotel bedrooms and stand up in overcrowded trains till I'm ready to drop, and what are you doing? Lounging about at home with your mouth open. Just look at me. Don't I look awful?"

"Terrible," said I. "You ought to take footbaths."

Damn it all, I thought. It's nice enough to have money but it seems to be a fearful fuss getting it.

I went to see Pigface. The train was so full it bulged. Many of the windows had no glass in them. Boards were nailed across instead. It stank horribly of old clothes and sweaty people. The air was filled with tobacco smoke and the smell of bad food. Even the lavatories were crammed with people.

They laughed at each other's jokes. By all means, sir, don't hold it in, but down wind, if you don't mind.

Some of the travelers, anxious to use the lavatories, were furious and said so. The others laughed at them. It was an endless journey.

When the train pulled into Frankfurt the carriages were cleared by policemen. Civilians in uniform drove the passengers on to the platform and searched their baggage. All food was confiscated, without compensation. The passengers on the platform yelled and screamed and tried to hang on to their food. A fat bitch with a silver cord around her hat was waving to a trainful of occupation troops just pulling out.

When our train moved on, the people weren't so noisy. They were thinking how they could get hold of something to feed their kids with, and about how bloody awful it is to lose a war. At Eichenberg the police cleared the train again.

I said to one of the coppers: "They already looted us in Frankfurt."

"Makes no difference," he said. "We'll still find several hundred pounds of grub. We're experts at it."

Nice crowd this, I thought, stealing the shirts off their countrymen's backs. But I didn't say so.

At Hanover a new lot was waiting for us.

"Come on, hand over the grub you've got hidden," said the policemen. "Before we tear the train to bits."

At Hamburg Central they were there again. They were more sympathetic, though.

"Bug off out of it," they said in their friendly fashion.

Pigface picked me up at the station. We didn't walk in step.

I said: "You wrote us a letter, about scrap metal. Bronze particularly. What's it all about?"

"Old church bells and smashed war memorials," whispered the former sergeant major.

"Man, that's the stuff," I said cheerfully. "But how are we going to move it to Bochum, which is where it's got to go? It's no use to us here."

"I've got a first-class man to handle that. A real expert," Pigface explained.

"Who is he? Anyone I know?" I asked.

"An old comrade-in-arms of ours. You'll have a fit when you see who it is," Pigface answered happily.

In the kitchen-living room sat the former divisional adjutant, Major Bredwitz. He was wearing a railwayman's uniform and he was eating bread and sausage.

"Well, if it isn't the general's flunky all dressed up in his new-found finery," he said with a grin. "Horlacher, if you'd stood under the Cross in that get-up and Jesus Christ had happened to look down, the whole course of history would have been changed! I'll say it would."

He laughed and laughed and laughed.

"I'm used to wearing a uniform, Major, I'm not built for civvy clothes."

"You can drop the major," Bredwitz snapped at me.

"Did you have it so bad in the Army you don't like to be reminded of it?" I asked.

"The Army was the tool of a criminal clique. I'd rather not remember that I ever took any part in the whole filthy business," the former adjutant snarled at me.

I said: "They gave me the run-around, but that doesn't mean I want to piss on my own doorstep."

"Horlacher, keep your trap shut!" roared Bredwitz. "I've known you for a long time. You're a typical thick-headed numbskull of an N.C.O. who lives his

life in blinders. A sexless wonder, that's what you are.
Neither a man nor a woman. If you don't like the way
you're treated you're the first to put up a howl, and
if you do you're only too happy to start the old barrel
organ going again. So much for that. Now let's talk
about the scrap. Where do you want it delivered?"

"How much does it cost?" I replied.

"I asked you where you wanted it delivered,"
snapped Bredwitz.

I said: "Bochum."

"We'll see it gets there. Just over one hundred tons
at the pre-war price. In exchange we'll want steel rope
and sheeting. We're going in for coal mining so as to
give our people something to eat. Meanwhile you can
cast new church bells and play carillons till you're blue
in the face for all I care. Here are the specifications of
what we want and the delivery dates," he said, pushing
a piece of paper toward me. "Our dear old sergeant
major and super-gaffer will act as contact man between
us and you. So go on home and let us know when
you want the first load of scrap delivered and who's
going to collect it."

"Where are we supposed to get this special steel
sheet and rope from?" I asked. "That sort of thing is
pretty well unobtainable these days."

"Is that your headache?" asked Bredwitz. "I thought
the general's daughter and her friend would be han-

dling that. By 'friend' I naturally mean the machine-tools manufacturer," he added with a grin.

"What are you trying to do? Set yourself up as managing director?" Pigface growled at me. "Put the piece of paper away in your pocket and give it to the general's daughter like a good little boy. That's all you've got to do."

"Can't waste any more time here," said Bredwitz, getting to his feet. He reached for his railwayman's cap.

"O.K., Horlacher," he said, "have a good trip home, and see you soon."

"I doubt very much if this deal will come off," I said.

The ex-sergeant major blew up at this point.

"God in heaven, you moron! Who the hell cares about what you doubt and what you don't doubt? Christ almighty!"

"Look," said the adjutant, "when you were a little boy your mummy sometimes used to give you a note and tell you to run around to the grocer's with it, didn't she? And you'd run off, and the grocer would give you what your mummy wanted, and you'd run home with it. Right?"

"Yes," I said.

"There you are," said he.

Supercilious bastard, I thought angrily. Who does

he think he is, talking to me like that? After all, he's only a railwayman now. It's not as though he was a major any more.

When he'd gone we made ourselves comfortable.

"Evi!" Pigface shouted at his wife. "Bring us the bottle and our breakfast."

She was a little black-haired piece with a wonderful chassis. She waggled her pretty little backside and I decided she'd be quite something in bed.

We stretched our legs, sitting on the sofa, and the ex-sergeant major pulled the cork from a bottle with a fancy label.

"We must drink to the deal," he said.

I said: "Cheers. One day we'll strike it rich."

I took a handsome swallow.

"Why don't you swap your scrap direct for mining equipment?" I asked. "It'd be much simpler for you."

"You talk as much sense as a pregnant virgin," grunted Pigface. "If they hear so much as a peep about us and our bronze we're in the cart once and for all. And all our friends with us. Nowadays a deal like that can only be done in Germany by the Yanks. They've got the proper business contacts and also the proper attitude toward making a little easy money. They give us exactly the equipment we want, out of confiscated property, you understand. They ship the bronze to

America for melting down. Or so they say. Actually they flog it to our foundries here in Germany. For the reconstruction of West German industry."

"The man who pays the piper calls the tune," remarked the general's daughter. "By exchanging scrap for steel rope and sheet we get a lot of stuff we need for our machine-tool factory. Whether or not it's legal is quite beside the point."

The front doorbell rang.

Now what? I thought. Who'd come and call on us? God almighty, it's probably the cops. I hurried to the door, but first I had a careful look through the slats of the Venetian blind. A woman was standing at the garden gate.

The general's daughter came running downstairs.

"I'll take care of this," she said.

When she walked back from the gate she was followed by a lady, a sour-faced old spinster by the look of her. Their heels clicked on the stone path. One of those distressed gentlewomen you read about, I thought.

She was the new housekeeper.

She began to spy on us right away.

I said to the general's daughter: "She seems a queer bird to me. Instead of grubbing about in our happy sex life, why doesn't the good lady do something about her halitosis?"

"We'll put a stop to her fun," the general's daughter promised. "I'm going to do some rebuilding and the first floor will be changed round. We'll have adjoining rooms, and then we'll be on our own. Incidentally, I'm clearing the distillery out of the cellar at the same time."

"You're getting rid of the still? You must be mad!"

"I've had enough of that racket," she said. "We've made plenty of money."

"Don't you believe it," said I. "A lot of water will flow under the bridge before Rentzsch's die stamps begin to roll off the assembly line."

Maybe what she needs is a decent drink, I thought, and I fetched a bottle and two glasses from the cupboard.

"We're starting with saucepans, not die stamps," the general's daughter explained. "And the sooner the factory begins working the better for us, because I've got the raw material and the orders too."

"What sort of raw material?"

"Fifty thousand German steel helmets, which are going to be saucepans," she said.

"Well, blow me down!" said I in amazement. "Where did you get the battle bowlers from? I thought the occupying people sat on all that sort of stuff as tight as a duck's arse."

I filled our glasses.

"I got them for a song. In fact they didn't cost me a penny," she assured me. "One night with an American major, that was all."

I wiped away a drop that was trickling down the neck of the bottle.

"You don't mind, do you, darling?"

Should I blow my top, or should I simply keep my trap shut? I just didn't know what I ought to do.

Rentzsch came.

He brought a builder-and-decorator with him, and they crawled all over the house, peering into every nook and cranny.

"Can't desist revisiting the scene of the crime, eh, Rentzsch?" I said.

He went quite gray.

"Horlacher, please don't make any more bad jokes," he whispered.

I said: "Don't worry. Our celebrated and highly solvent schnapps company was wound up day before yesterday and the machinery dismantled. What remains of it is stacked in the toolshed at the bottom of the garden. If you like you can take it away and raffle it at a bazaar for the undernourished offspring of the occupation forces."

Rentzsch gave a sigh of relief.

"I'll see that the gear disappears at once," he said. "We'll take it to the factory and throw it on the scrap heap. While the building is going on there'll be a lorry traveling regularly back and forth. So it'll be easy to move it."

"Building? I thought it was only a question of making a few alterations to the happy home."

Rentzsch was whistling thoughtfully between his teeth. He stood in the garden and stared up at the general's love nest. Like an admiral on the high seas, just before he gives the order to open fire.

Good luck to you, you poor old house, I thought. And sighed.

We were at breakfast.

"When your old man comes home and sees what we've done to this shack of his, he won't half tear a strip off us," I said.

The general's daughter was reading her mail.

I tapped the top of an egg and placed it in front of her. The distressed gentlewoman brought in the coffee, and took the chance to give me a good long stare.

Sometimes I felt I could lose my temper with that down-at-heel duchess.

"Another letter from Olten," said the general's daughter.

"He must be in a bad way then," I said.

"Father always thought a lot of him. I'd like to find him a job in the factory, to tide him over."

"Don't do it," I said. "Olten's quite capable of turning the factory into a divisional headquarters before you can say Jack Robinson. The workers would mutiny," I said. "I think that's a rotten idea."

"What do you mean, *you* think it's a rotten idea? I decide what happens in the factory. Let's get that straight once and for all."

I said: "It's not only your money, you know. I put my earnings into the concern as well."

"*What!* That takes the biscuit!"

I could see she was very angry.

"Fifty-fifty," I said.

"I work myself to a standstill, and you think you should take half the profits? Are you absolutely mad?"

"Honey, there's a nasty streak of pride in your character," I said. "We brewed schnapps together, we share the profits."

"You're a useless idiot," she said between her teeth.

"And don't try to swindle me," I said, "because I'm not standing for it."

"Your love of money has made you lose your senses," she shouted. "You're behaving worse than a Jew."

She jumped up. Her chair fell over.

"I never thought much of your character," she said, "but I hadn't expected that you'd sacrifice what limited sense of loyalty you have just for the love of money. Well, maybe it's a good thing that my eyes should be opened now, before it's too late."

She was fuming.

"This row is quite pointless," I said. "You've got to swallow the pill, no matter how nasty it tastes."

"You bastard," she snarled.

"And to hell with your steel helmet saucepans," I said. "As far as I'm concerned you can brew yourself a nice glass of vitriol in them."

"We'll have to get a car," the general's daughter said. "We live in the Black Forest and the factory is in Esslingen. I can't go back and forth by train indefinitely."

"Wouldn't you find driving all that way a bit of a strain in the long run, too?" I asked.

"Got any more brilliant ideas? Do you think I'm planning to drive myself?"

"Nothing surprises me any more," I said. "It sounds

as though you've already decided what sort of a chauffeur's uniform you're going to put me in."

"I thought you'd look terribly sweet in navy blue. Double-breasted. Would you like that, darling?"

She smiled, so that her teeth showed.

The American car was magnificent. She had bought it second-hand. The man who sold it to us assured us that a famous dance-band singer had conceived her first child on the back seat.

I said: "We're not superstitious," and steered the hundred and thirty-five chromium-plated horses straight at a crowd of my fellow men. Makes their lives a little less dull, jumping about a bit like that.

The general's daughter sat beside me, observing the landscape.

"Why do you store all your saucepans and kettles and whatever else it is you make? You've got sheds full of the stuff. Why don't you unload the junk on your buyer as quick as ever you can?" I asked.

"That stock is our capital," she said. "We're hoarding it. We only sell as much as we need to keep the business going. When the Americans have invested enough money in western Germany to stabilize the mark, we'll get rid of our stock, but not a minute before."

"Extraordinary how good at business you've turned out to be," I said.

"Lots of people are," she said. "The only difference is that most people don't get a chance to show it."

"That's fate," said I.

She opened her handbag. From among the collection of junk which she always carried—lipstick, compact, cigarette case and heaven knows what else—she extracted a letter. There was a French stamp on the envelope.

"From Bordeaux," said the general's daughter, tapping the letter with her fingertips. She pinched me gently in the ribs.

We were driving through the Swabian Alb. Pines and firs hemmed in the narrow roads that twisted over the mountains, down to the Danube, which flows so swiftly, because it has to pass through Germany.

ROCKETS were going off. Through the woods there re-echoed the cheers of the populace. The hillside was black with people. The crowds stretched down to the edge of the road which ran along the valley. Flags fluttered in the breeze. Women held bunches of flowers in their hands. Fathers carried their younger children pick-a-back. The Rifle Club band played a succession of patriotic hymns and anthems.

Very erect, hat in hand, the general strode along the path that led to his house. The delegation which had met the car tactfully remained behind. Only the general's daughter accompanied him, two yards behind her father and to one side.

Straight as a ramrod, a picture of dignity, the general marched through the crowd.

Women sobbed. The men's expression was one of firmness and determination. Children were wide-eyed with wondering awe. To the roll of drums the band broke into the German National Anthem. It was a paean of thanksgiving. The general was home.

"God be with you," he grunted, and strode through the garden gate.

"Good morning, sir," said I.

"What the devil have you been doing to my tomatoes?" he snapped, and his eyes moved round the garden. "Why are they all leaning over sideways?"

I said: "I was told it was better for them that way, sir. They'll give a bigger crop."

"People will tell you anything," growled the general. "Which is no reason why my tomatoes should loll about the place like drunken sailors. The first thing you do tomorrow is to straighten them up again. In line, the way they ought to be. Understand?"

"Yes, sir."

I thought, I only hope he won't run amok.

The house was a shining apparition of elegance and fresh paint. There were wrought-iron gates and a low wall, which hadn't been there before, not to mention a decorative lantern above the front door. Windows and doors were of gleaming new wood, and the old toolshed had been changed into a low building incorporating a garage.

The general was flabbergasted. A screech from the distressed gentlewoman brought him back to reality.

"Welcome home!" she yelled.

Just like a stationmaster shouting: All aboard! Stand clear of the doors! The general's face assumed an expression of delight. Jovially, he held out his hand.

"My daughter has already told me about your existence," he said. "I'm very pleased to have such a worthy addition to my household."

The distressed gentlewoman's eyes almost popped out of her head for pride. The general's face, which had been thrust forward, returned to the as-you-were position, his chin resting on his collar, and he marched on. He went indoors.

I showed the general his new bedroom with the adjoining study.

I had disinterred the diaries buried in the forest and placed them on his desk. Maps of the countries adjoining Germany, together with a large-scale map of Germany itself, covered most of the walls. But a place of honor had been reserved for the general's favorite picture, *The Madonna with the Canary*. The general's small and carefully selected library was set out in a glass-fronted bookcase.

There were photographs everywhere: the general as cadet, subaltern, lieutenant, captain and so on. It was thus possible to take in the general's professional career at a single glance.

The desk, by the window, was perfectly equipped. In a long and shallow dish lay pencils, both black and colored, all the same length, all sharpened to a fine point. There was a calendar, in- and out-baskets, an address book, a magnifying glass, even a pencil, all was ready. A desk fit for a general.

The general's daughter and I had taken great pains to ensure that the returning general would find the sort of surroundings to which he had been accustomed during his long and distinguished military career.

A barometer hung beside the study window. A photograph of the general's lady was prominently displayed upon the desk. A shell fragment, which had nearly caught the general's head during the course of the First World War and which now acted as a paperweight, lay conveniently to hand. From a steel peg hung the flyswatter made of hairs from Petrus's tail.

That was the name of the horse which had carried the general through tournaments in years gone by.

The general examined everything. Thoroughly.

I waited by the door which connected bedroom and study, half expecting to hear a bellow of rage. But I saw the general run his hand over the top of the desk, gaze affectionately at the photo of his wife, thumb rapidly through one of the diaries, and I realized with relief that the general was satisfied with the preparations we had made for his homecoming.

The difference between this carefully ordered room and a prison cell was, after all, pretty striking.

I went into the bathroom and ran water into the tub. I tossed in a couple of pine-scented bath cubes and the sweet smell of resin spread rapidly. It reached the general's nose, and he began to sniff happily.

"Wonderful smell, that," he said, and walked into the bathroom.

He dipped one finger into the greenish water.

"Exactly seventy degrees, sir," I reported.

"Let's go up to seventy-two," he ordered.

I ran in a little more hot.

"Nothing better for the health than a nice hot bath," sand the general, and began to undress. He picked up the soap and sniffed at it. Then he hopped into the tub.

His body was emaciated. The cushion of fat about his knees had vanished and the bones stuck out. His skin had a disagreeable look to it, like goose flesh. He was an old man.

I scrubbed the general with the long-handled brush, using a lot of soap, then sprayed him with the hand shower till his hide shone. The general grunted with pleasure.

Well, old boy, how do you feel now? I thought. Now that you've got a lovely, well-arranged life again?

The general was playing with the nailbrush, seeing if it could carry the weight of the soap. It couldn't, the soap tipped off, and the general scrabbled about on the bottom of the tub till he found it again.

"My daughter seems to be financially all right," he said, blowing water from his nose.

I said: "Fräulein von Puckhammer has done very well indeed in business, sir."

"She told me something about a machine-tool factory," the general said. "I wonder if that's quite suitable an occupation for a young lady? What sort of a concern is it? I mean, is it likely to provide a decent livelihood more or less permanently?"

"Undoubtedly, sir. At least so long as your daughter has the final say in the way it's run. Which she has now."

The general was clearing water from his ear, using his little finger for the purpose.

"If this machine-tool business is really so reliable, I suppose I can pursue my professional career without having to worry about financial matters?" he said.

"That is exactly the idea, sir," said I.

The general could have jumped for joy. He stared happily at his sponge, which was slowly becoming water-logged, until it sank below the surface.

The general soon became accustomed to his new way of life. As always we rose early. Why the devil can't the old man lie in till ten? I thought. As a general (Retd.) that was quite out of the question. I woke him.

"Good morning, sir. It looks like a fine day today," I reported. "But the radio gave out thunder for later on."

"Bad for the mosquitoes, and good for the cucumbers," the general remarked cheerfully.

He got up and went to the bathroom. He had his morning bath, followed by his breakfast.

"Is the wreath for the war memorial ready?" he asked.

"Yes, sir. A beautiful wreath, oak leaves, with a black, white and red ribbon. Just as the general ordered."

"What a lovely morning," he said, and stared out of the window.

"It's the anniversary of the day the general's division broke the Metaxas Line," I said.

"Which resulted in the encirclement of the whole of the Greek Epirus-Macedonian army," announced the general, and sipped at his coffee. "If the English hadn't hung on so stubbornly at Thermopylae, that would never have happened to the Greeks."

The general's head was slightly on one side and he smiled nostalgically.

"Those were lovely days, down in Greece," he murmured.

He rolled up his napkin.

"Well, duty before pleasure," he growled, and got to his feet.

I helped him into his coat. I accompanied him as far as the garden gate.

I watched him for a while as he made his way, on his thin legs, down the path across the meadow. The wreath hung from his right arm. He would place it at the foot of the war memorial, remove his hat, and remember the Metaxas Line. And the many decorations which that battle had won him. Later he would slowly climb the hill again. The general made many such excursions these days.

The calendar was covered with reminders of anniversaries.

I had opened an account with a florist who supplied the wreaths. That was one of my jobs.

I was waiting for the general, down on the road. We walked back to the house together. Past the orchards where peach trees were trained to stakes, and rusting iron netting hung down the walls. Sometimes we would stop.

The general breathed deeply and I noticed the banks of cloud which were rearing up above the Black Forest. We could feel the wind from off the mountains. We watched the flocks of starlings.

"How can a flock of starlings turn and wheel so quickly, without the birds ever colliding?" the general asked. "Which one gives the order for the maneuver?" he wanted to know.

I could see that he was puzzled.

"No bomber squadron could ever change direction with the speed and precision of these starlings. You notice that each individual bird keeps the same position in the ranks. Whether it's done as a platoon or in divisional strength, they never make a mistake. You won't catch one of them treading on the heels of the man in front! And at a flying speed of twenty yards per second. How do the starlings manage it? Most remarkable!"

Swallows came gliding down the hillside. They flew low along the walls, like fighter-bombers along a road. We walked slowly on.

"One of these starlings would die of old age in the time it takes us to teach a recruit, on the barrack square, the difference between right and left," said the general. "How is it that they can drill so well without ever being trained? There's something wrong there."

The general was sunk deep in thought.

"Every drill sergeant knows what a business it is to teach recruits any complicated drill movement. The first rank marks time till the others have done the turn and caught up. Easy enough, you'd think. But by the time the men have learned it their first year's service is over," the general said.

His chalky old face was raised toward the starlings. To hell with the birds, thought I.

"A good animal psychologist should be able to explain why the starlings are capable of carrying out such extremely complicated drill movements with such apparent ease," said the general.

I looked at the cloud bank. It was light gray, growing steadily darker, and was in striking contrast to the forests still in sunshine on the hilltops. In front of this backdrop the starlings wheeled and turned, providing fuel for the general's mental processes.

Each day the general attended a solitary situation conference.

"The 10th U.S.A.F. Tactical Reconnaissance Wing is moving from Bavaria to the Soissons-Rheims area," he would read aloud from his newspaper. "That's excellent," he would say, and stick a colored pin into one of his maps.

"The 117th Tactical Bomber Squadron, R.A.F., is being transferred to the Toul area," the general would announce, and another pin of another color would go into the map at the appropriate spot. Then he would take a step back and examine the overall effect.

He would read on:

"The Royal Air Force are moving their base depots from Germany to Holland, where they will be established in the Scheldt area. The French Air Force are moving the 3rd Escadrille-de-Chasse from the Friedrichshafen area to the area Besançon-Dijon, while the Rastatt depots are being transferred to Nancy." All such reports were immediately marked up on the general's maps.

He enjoyed this daily chore. Even in civilian life the

general was a hard-working man. Every day he worked to a fixed schedule. At least one hour was devoted to an intensive examination of the measures being taken by his foreign colleagues. The necessary intelligence for this study he gleaned from the daily papers.

"The commander of the Southern Sector of N.A.T.O., after discussions with the French authorities and with Italian military leaders, has agreed that the stocks of war materials at present located on the Italian mainland in the Leghorn area shall be transferred at once to the island of Corsica."

Then the general heaved a sigh of relief.

"At last!" he murmured. "It was absolutely insane leaving all that valuable equipment at the mercy of an unreliable civilian population. There's no telling what might have happened to it, if the balloon had gone up." With evident delight the general moved one large pin from Leghorn to Corsica.

Meanwhile I entered these developments in the special card index which the general had created for the purpose.

"The Spanish government has announced its agreement that certain essential French supply depots be transferred to Spanish territory," the general announced. "Extremely interesting," he murmured. "Horlacher, do you realize what that means?"

"No, sir."

"It means that in case things get serious, we'll have the Pyrenees as a rear covering line, and the area as far as the Elbe will therefore be freed for a war of maneuver."

The general was deeply impressed by this revelation.

"There are all sorts of strategic possibilities," he cried enthusiastically, and his hands zigzagged across the map of Europe. "Here and here there'll be combat groups of our allies, to which let us hope German forces will soon be added. That means we can create three hedgehogs. We can reckon on at least four hedgehogs in France. The mouth of the Scheldt is sealed off. Likewise the Cotentin. All these hedgehogs will have to be equipped on a somewhat modest scale, since everything they'll need must be stored beforehand in deep, bomb-proof shelters. So far as possible the hedgehogs must be set up in difficult country, preferably in the mountains. One in the Swabian Alb, another in the Eifel, which means the third will have to be in the Kaiserslautern area. Each hedgehog should cover between fifteen and thirty square miles of terrain. The civilian populations must be issued with identification discs, which they'll have to carry at all times. Each disc should show the person's number, religion, blood group, together with a microfilm of his identity card, behind a plastic shield which won't splinter in case of atomic bombing. Then we'll be able to identify the corpses. When the shooting starts the Italians will be responsible for holding the line Genoa-Bologna-Rimini, at least for a while. The Dutch and Danish armed forces will form hedgehogs. In Spain there'll be a highly trained and extremely well equipped assault army standing ready, partly to act as a fire brigade but chiefly for use at a later stage of the war. That is to say, an offensive force capable of attacking toward eastern Europe when wanted, though of course it would have to move north to start with. Good God, man, think of the freedom of maneuver! I could jump for joy at the very thought! With a mere hundred divisions one could have a really fascinating war!"

The general was standing, arms akimbo, gazing at his wall maps.

"Now let's take it the other way about," he said, furrowing his brow. "Let us assume that I am the Russian chief of staff. What would I do when confronted with a situation such as this?"

The general stroked his chin.

"First of all, England must disappear," he said. "It's a base for counterattacks, and as such must be wiped out at once. A hail of rockets must be launched against the island fortress. Next, knock out America as a world power. So pulverize the coasts of the U.S.A. by means of rockets and submarines."

The general turned on his heel and stared out of the

window. Meanwhile I was reading the motto pinned over his desk.

The best strategy is to protract operations until such time as the enemy's morale has reached a point at which it is not only possible but comparatively easy to deal him a fatal blow.

The general had constructed a sand table in the garden. Mixing fact with fantasy, he carried out an elaborately planned exercise. I had to take a hand in this.

The "Reds" had once again infuriated the "Whites." The general had therefore felt obliged, during the previous week, to issue the orders for general mobilization. The relevant documents lay on his desk. The "Reds" had called up their chaps at the same time, needless to say. At the moment their troops were occupying, in the sand table, various points west of the Weser. Even though the general had naturally blown all the bridges to smithereens the moment the war began. He was now sending his "White" armored divisions to attack my "Red" assault troops.

I threw beans at them, and the sand flew. The general hurled a couple of tomatoes into my area. They hit an engineer battalion and an infantry regiment.

"That was the atomic artillery," announced the general.

All the same, my "Red" tanks managed to push on, straight through the general's divisions. They were headed for Bad Pyrmont and points west. Straight for the parsley which grew on the far side of the sand table.

The general planted an extensive minefield of spring onions, just in front of his forward defensive line, and my combat groups were forced to make a lengthy detour, which wasted a lot of time, particularly since more minefields were constantly springing up, which meant more changes of direction. All this was necessary in order to give the general the time he needed to withdraw his "White" troops into their hedgehogs.

Then he allowed me two tomatoes. I threw them both at the "White" hedgehogs. Immediately after this the "Red" and the "White" tanks bumped each other, slap in the middle of the Lüneburg Heath, and a terrific slaughter began.

The general bombarded my part of the sand table with beans and green plums, which were supposed to represent bombs. I regrouped my forces. The general felt compelled to break off the engagement.

The reserves at his disposal weren't enough to make a single "Red" soldier spit out a single sunflower seed.

"I shall have to devote considerable thought to the battle situation and the lessons to be learned from this exercise," the general announced.

He stared across the garden. Across the flowerbeds,

where the flowers grew straight as guardsmen, across the tidy paths and the well-clipped lawn.

The paving stones which led up to the front door were embedded in moss. Beside the path, at regular intervals, there bloomed a lovely rose. Brightly colored carnations were grouped about the birdbath. The watering cans, arranged by size, were scrubbed till they shone, and in the red-cabbage patch the scarecrows wore polished boots.

I was unrolling the hose from off its drum, for it was time to water the plants.

"Our tactics are out of date," said the general. "There's no sense in shelling the infantry with high explosive any more. Nothing but a waste of time. Thermonuclear bombs and shells are what we need. A good barrage, raising the air temperature to several thousand degrees, and within a split second you'll have dealt with the lot of them."

The general was spraying the garden. He wore a light linen suit and a broad-brimmed panama hat. He was smoking an excellent cigar, and from the nozzle of his hose a steady shower rose to fall again upon the flowerbeds.

"Lice infected with typhus—drop millions and millions of them on the enemy's cities. And atom bombs in cargo ships. Sink the ships in the enemy's ports before the outbreak of war and then set them off at the proper time by remote control," said the general.

"Or scatter radioactive dust from high-flying planes into air currents which would carry the dust to the enemy's country. Long-range rockets could fire loads of Colorado beetle and other such pests. Then there are cholera-infected rats which could be smuggled in. And locusts could be used to spread various plant diseases."

The general turned his spray on the herb bed and the irises.

I carried the hose across the lawn, taking good care not to twist it or to damage the flowers.

"The ideal thing might be meteorological warfare," the general was saying. "By scattering silver iodite it should be possible to cause such storms that the enemy would be bogged down and his tanks and supply columns totally immobilized. Or even disappear in the mud. Convoys and warships could be protected by artificial fogs. While clouds over bomb targets could be rapidly dissipated. A great advantage to us would be the fact that the prevailing winds move eastward. All this confronts the meteorologists with tasks which they must solve in the immediate future."

The general walked across to the vegetable garden. His artificial and beneficent rain poured down upon the cabbages, which had never looked healthier.

"Wonderful display," remarked the general happily, pointing at the vegetables. "We've got the marvelous weather of the last few weeks to thank for this."

He pushed his hat on to the back of his head.

"You know, Horlacher," he said. "Whenever I come out here and look at all this, I have to admit that I've been extraordinarily fortunate in my life. To be able to enjoy a lovely house, a beautiful garden, a wonderful view, and above all . . ."

He stared at a butterfly, sipping a flower, and his thoughts were far away.

That evening there were guests.

Colonel Olten, and the former garrison commander with his wife. The director of the theatre, now re-opened, had also been invited: as well as the professor from the nearby university.

"I came across a most interesting case recently," said the professor. "A Bohemian corporal who'd gone off his nut, gave an Italian salute, wore an American uniform, and said he was Chancellor of Germany."

I grinned politely and helped him off with his coat.

At dinner the wife of the former garrison commander was holding forth:

"He said that the German people, tempered in the crucible of the recent war, were predestined to lead

Europe and to save her, because the other nations are degenerate and flabby. But our nation has been toughened by battle, which is why we are the only people who can stand up to the East."

The lady spoke rather more rapidly than in the old days.

"The belief that the Western Powers alone are capable of throwing back an attack on western Europe is unfortunately no longer a tenable hypothesis. That's what he said," she went on. "Which is why a German defense contribution is now essential."

"It'll come," the general assured her. "You can rely on one thing: the soldiers will soon be back. And when we are, we shall be tough and relentless, which will be all to the good."

"For us Germans the Army is one of the pillars of the State, erected by God's will," said the former garrison commander. "Like agriculture and the churches."

"How happy I should be to put on uniform again," announced Olten. "I'm afraid I'm like the leopard. As my friends will tell you, I can't change my spots."

"Nobody can," said the general. "And no sensible person would ever expect anyone to try. Just wait a little while, till our politicians begin asking the old questions about guns or butter. You'll get your wish all right then."

"I hope the re-establishment of the West German armed forces won't lead to trouble with the Russians," said the director.

"I can't see that that matters," said the general. "By then the new German age groups will be fit for service, and our old soldiers will still be able to teach them a thing or two. Also I strongly suspect that our women, now that they have equal rights, will adopt the attitude, in a case of crisis, that it's an honor to bear arms for one's country. I wouldn't be surprised if they demanded the right to fight shoulder-to-shoulder beside their menfolk."

After dinner the gentlemen played cards and the ladies drank liqueurs.

"How is your factory doing?" the wife of the former garrison commander asked.

"Very well indeed, thank you," said the general's daughter, unscrewing her lipstick. "We're just about to start manufacturing steel helmets."

It was night.

The general's daughter and I were lying, half-undressed, on the sofa. We were drinking rum and the general's daughter was telling me about her father: about his education at the cadet school, the drill, and his teachers who all wore monocles. Then there was his time as an ensign of cavalry, and the unfortunate scandal in which he was involved with his commanding officer's wife. She spoke of five-gaited horses and reviews and church parades and a couple of pale-faced girls of excellent family. The money: sometimes he would wash his horses in champagne: sometimes he'd have his camp bed set up right in the stables, so that even in the dark he could reach out and grab hold of horseflesh. Then came Eleonore, who was to be the general's wife. She was very much out of the top drawer.

The general's daughter spoke of garrison duty and regiments, of orders and decorations. The general was mentioned in dispatches and never lost his faith in God. She spoke of bugle calls and neighing horses and of the night when the general had made his soldiers sing the bridal chorus from *Lohengrin* while a steaming stallion served his mare. The general had scattered his seed, had created soldiers to fight for his country and, of course, had fought himself. He had signed death warrants and had always loved Germany above all else.

With astonishment I realized that he had not actually been born a general. We'd made him one.

THE former members of the general's division were celebrating a reunion.

The little town was decorated with flags and flowers. Fresh greenery hung from the house fronts. Gardens were neatly hoed and at the tables outside the inns beer mugs clinked.

On the evening before the reunion there was a dinner at a respectable hotel attended by those officers who had once served in the division and who still happened to be alive. There were handshakes and toasts and a first-class meal.

While coffee was being served one of the officers persuaded Colonel Olten to sit down on a chair which made a loud noise, like a fart.

The former officers were up to all sorts of merry pranks, and it wasn't long before most of them were stinking.

"Come on, obstacle race!" shouted the former divisional paymaster. The whole crowd began galloping about, seated astride their chairs. They lumbered from room to room, up the stairs, and through the guests' bedrooms, shouting and laughing. Chairs splintered and smashed. The whole mob roared and stumbled through the lavatories and corridors and back to the dining room. They clinked glasses and sang dirty songs. "Who knows Goliath the Giant, the strongest man in the world . . . ?"

"Those poor fellows are terrified they'll die of boredom as civilians," I explained to the waiter. "You mustn't mind their bit of fun."

"My dear fellow," he replied, "this sort of thing means nothing to me. I'm a pacifist."

Next morning the former divisional chaplain celebrated mass in the church. Candles flickered. There were fourteen pictures, in medieval style, upon the walls. They depicted Christ's Stages of the Cross. Beginning with His reception by the "High Commissar," and on to the bitter end.

Bells were rung.

In a side chapel Saint Barbara stood upon a gold-embroidered cloth and smiled amiably at the many strange men who filled the pews and aisles, discussing their sins with the Almighty Himself.

Shadows moved across the brightly painted roof. There was the smell of incense. The chaplain sang out, in his beer-barrel bass: *"Dominus vobiscum!"*

Two communicants, dressed as N.C.O.s and peering around at the general who was seated in the front row, tripped on the altar steps. The general had already attended the Protestant service. Now he was honoring the Catholic survivors of his division with his presence. The Devotions ended with a silent prayer for the souls of fallen comrades.

This reunion of old soldiers had got off to a proper and dignified start.

I drove the general to the tent on the Rifle Club's ground. Olten was in the car, together with the former adjutant. I'd fixed up the general's old standard on the front of the bonnet. People in the streets, and the policemen, saluted in the proper way.

In fact it was just like the old days.

I parked the car and walked across to a sausage counter, where Pigface was waiting for me. From a nearby tent came the strains of a march.

"Who'd have thought it," said Pigface. 'There's some of them still in P.O.W. camps and us here starting a soldiers' society called THRUST AND PARRY."

"Give me a sausage too," I said to the old woman who was stoking her woodburner on the other side of the counter.

A former M.P. who'd once been in the same company as me, came across to us.

"Well, I am a fool," he said, "not to have recognized you right away."

I remarked to Pigface: "He's the sort hangs on to his musket so tight they have to bury it with him."

The ex-sergeant major ordered more sausages.

"What have you been up to these last few years?" he asked our old pal.

"Having a holiday in Russia," he said. Holding the sausage in his crippled hand, he dipped it in the mustard. "Had a hell of a time," he added.

"Well, it's all over now," I said by way of cheering him up.

"If only we hadn't started that bloody war, I'd have been spared a lot," he said with a grin. "Ivan gave me the run-around, I can tell you. Make your hair stand on end. I used to think, if only I could be sure they'd ship my coffin home. I didn't fancy being thrown on to one of them Russian boneheaps."

"How many Russkis had you rubbed out then?" I asked.

"Hard to say exactly. We didn't keep records much you know, and there was such a lot of them. Particularly when we were running the Napoleon Memorial Stakes."

"You were bloody lucky Ivan didn't find out about your job," said I. "You'd better be thankful for that and forget the rest. And if anyone ever tries to get you for what you did, you just come and see our general here. He'll give you a certificate saying you only ever murdered and hanged people because you were ordered to do so."

"That's right, and it's damn true," said the former

M.P. "Why else should I go around stringing people up? I was brought up in a decent, God-fearing home. They forced me into it. My duty, that's what they said it was."

"O.K. That puts paid to that," I said. "Otherwise, how's things, you old scrounger?"

"Can't seem to get me a girl," he said.

The din inside the tent was ear-splitting. The former soldiers were seated at long tables. The former officers were at other tables, at right angles to the soldiers. They could look at the men they used to command.

"A superb opportunity for observation," Olten was saying to the general. "I'm amazed what a magnificent job our men can do, showing the civilians what a civilian suit can be made to look like!"

Waitresses with rolled up sleeves were passing out plates of bacon and beans. Cigarette and ice-cream vendors circled the tables. Various colored flags hid the holes in the canvas. In huge white letters a banner proclaimed: TO BE A GERMAN IS TO BE TRUE. Underneath it was the exit to the latrines. Men waved to one another.

At one table they were singing: "One starry night on the Russian front, a-thinking of my . . ."

At the officers' table the general was saying excitedly: "For me, a democrat is a man who was pleased to see our Greater German Reich occupied by the enemy and hundreds of thousands of his compatriots expelled from their homes." He went on: "And nowadays, when I have to watch the sort of politics these gentry are playing, my gorge rises, I can tell you."

A former captain glanced at his watch.

"Don't you agree, general," he said, getting to his feet, "that we must devote all our energies to industry and commerce these days?"

"By all means, my friend," replied the general, "devote your energies wherever you see fit. But don't forget what you learned in the Army, and don't talk too much."

The former captain clicked his heels. The general politely raised his backside a half-inch from the seat of his chair. Then he leaned back comfortably again, put his fingers together, and began to twiddle his thumbs.

With a piercing voice, trained to carry across several barrack squares, the captain shouted: "Comrades!"

The din inside the tent subsided.

"Comrades! Today the members of our division are celebrating our reunion in this worthy town, famous in history and in song! The town councillors, headed by his worship the mayor, and all the administrative services have done all in their power to make our stay here a pleasant one. I want to express the heartiest thanks of all of us to them for what they've done! May these happy hours bring us old soldiers closer together and make us ever more determined to fulfill our willing obligations to those comrades who made the supreme sacrifice or who are missing. These hours of gay reunion are also a testimony to the fact that in spirit and attitude we are the same men we were at the front in years gone by. By which I mean that we are Germans! That we are obedient! And that we know how to fight!"

Thunderous applause roared out.

"Comrades," shouted the former captain, "pray silence for our general whom we all honor and respect, and who is now going to say a few words to you."

The applause was even more thunderous than before.

A happy smile was playing about the general's lips. Nimbly he threaded his way among the chairs. When he was standing in front of the tables, he visibly drew himself up to his full height and thrust out his chest. He raised his hand for silence.

"Germany, land of our fathers," he bellowed. "Land of green forests and flowering meadows and fields, land of silent lakes. . . ." His voice had dropped dramatically, but it was still quite plainly audible.

The general paused to let his words take their full effect. The waitress put another pot of beer in front of me.

"Let us give thanks to our Maker that we were born in this land," shouted the general. "That we may say with pride: 'This is our country, the country for which we fought.' It does not matter who won. No, comrades! All that matters is that we fought the good fight, like good soldiers, and obeyed our orders!"

The general's voice changed gear.

"Shame on those dishonorable scoundrels who will not bow down before the tale of duty willingly performed and sacrifice nobly endured by our heroic soldiers!"

There was harshness in the general's tone. His words rang through the tent.

"Politics at this moment are as remote to us as the man in the moon," the general stated. "But that doesn't mean that we're a pack of patient sheep, ready to put up with anything those scoundrels may try to do to us. Far from it. The time is fast approaching when we shall know how to deal with that traitorous gang which finds such satisfaction in sneering at Germany's soldiers. When that time comes we'll use every weapon at our disposal."

The general's eyes were shining.

"Comrades!" screamed the general. "Close your

ranks! The time has come to speak out loud and clear!
The days when they could degrade us as criminals are
over and done with! Thanks to the praiseworthy attitude of our people and the far-sighted political actions
of our worthy statesmen!"

"Goddammit!" whispered Pigface, who was seated
beside me. "He's really pouring it on."

I said: "A good speech, eh? The old man spent a
tremendous amount of time over it. It took him weeks
to learn it by heart."

The general spoke at length and in detail.

Finally he said: "When we leave this place and
separate, each to return to his family and his place of
work, every one of us must take with him the deepest
determination to work together for the reconstruction
of our Fatherland. And each of us in his daily words
and deeds must be a living witness to the honor of
having once been a German soldier. Let this be your
watchword. Let each of you strive fanatically to hasten
the day when there will once again be a German army
which can march openly through our streets! If we live
and work with this one object in mind, then the happy
day will come when we can look back with pride on a
task attempted and a task achieved. Nor will that day
now be long delayed. There are certain among us
gathered together here who on that day will have the
supreme honor of donning the finest garment to which

a German can aspire, I mean the soldier's tunic!"

"M.P.s will be back in fashion then too," said the former M.P. cheerfully.

An ex-sergeant said: "I wonder if they'd take me back? I collected fifteen wounds but I can still button my own pants."

We stood up. We sang the *Comrades' Song:*

"Ich hatt' einen Kameraden, einen bessern find'st du nicht. Die Trommel schlug zum Streite, er ging an meiner Seite, im gleichen Schritt und Tritt. . . ."

At the next table a man suddenly gave vent to a raucous laugh. Well, blow me down, I thought. The man must be tight.

We sang:

"Eine Kugel kam geflogen, gilt sie dir oder gilt sie mir? Ihn hat es weggerissen. . . ."

"And how!" guffawed the fellow at the next table.

"Throw him out!" shouted the ex-M.P.

Someone tried to grab the heckler by the throat. The man was trembling with rage.

"Don't you see it's all a lot of hooey!" he shouted. "Won't you bone-headed Teutons ever realize when you're being led around by the nose? Are you going to let the warmongers put you back in the shafts all over again? So as the corpse dealers can grow nice and fat?"

Heads were punched. Chaos broke out.

"Do you want to see Germany all smashed up again?" roared the agitator.

"Damned swine, SHUT UP!" shouted the ex-sergeant.

"You sing about hell happily enough. And you'd run a man in for giving his poodle a clip on the ear."

"I know who that loony is," cried a legless man. "The Army gave him every medal in the shop, including the Close Combat Clasp in Silver."

"Comrades, keep your heads! Don't let him start a fight!" shouted the captain from the officers' table. "Chuck the fellow out! Give him some fresh air!"

A group of men grabbed him and tossed him out of the tent. Then we sang on.

That evening they blew retreat, with all the trimmings. Drums and bugles and hats off for prayers. The band blasted away by torchlight. In front of the town hall, and in the sidestreets, silent crowds watched this moving spectacle of a living German tradition. Their emotions subsided only when the band, having played the National Anthem, marched off to the beat of martial music.

To top it all off, there was a big reception at the hotel.

The general said: "A man must be an extraordinarily vulgar blackguard to interrupt the finest soldier's song we Germans possess by shouting defeatist propaganda slogans. We must root out such poisonous weeds before they carry their infection any further."

"There should be a law. Swines like that ought to be declared outlaws," suggested a former captain.

"It's high time we made a bit of a stir," said Olten, "and showed the criminal elements among the youth of Germany which way the wind is blowing."

"They may talk peace propaganda outside the barrack gates now. Just let 'em wait till we've got them inside!" announced the general. "We'll give those lads such a chasing, they'll be happy to die at the front and the sooner the better. Meanwhile our decent young men will get an intensive training lasting at least two years, so that they become tough and reliable soldiers. Men who can march and fight. They must learn beyond question that their job is in the workshops of death, that their duty is to kill and to be killed. We must drum into their heads that the German soldier willingly abandons his right to live, together with all our civilian privileges. We don't want a lot of parade-ground tin soldiers, what we need are fearless and skillful fighting men. Because war is coming."

"Did you say war, sir?" asked Bredwitz. "Surely nobody expects that."

"Who's been leading you up the garden path?" sneered the general, looking at the captain with irritation. "There always have been wars, and there always will be. Just think back: 1920 to 1949, civil war in China. Nineteen hundred thirty-one and 1932, the Japanese conquest of Manchuria, followed by the Abyssinian war and the Spanish civil war. Nineteen hundred thirty-seven to 1938, the war between Japan and China. Nineteen hundred thirty-nine and 1940, the Russo-Finnish war. Then the Second World War, followed by civil war in Greece. From 1946 to 1954 continuous fighting in French Indo-China. Nineteen hundred forty-eight and 1949, war between Israel and the Arab States, and then the balloon went up in Korea. The guns will be firing again soon, mark my words. My friend, there's one thing you can rely on: peace hasn't got a hope any longer! The greatest war of all time is coming. Atomic mushrooms will sprout in the skies; the rivers and oceans will boil; the earth will rumble and quake; the fields and meadows will be deep in ashes. A deadly rain will drop from the clouds; no birds will sing; the whole world will fester with poison and filth; and everywhere tongues of consuming flame will leap up." The general was shouting now. "Cowards will creep into caves and holes in the ground," he went on. "But proper men will fight and die! Bravely, knowing in their hearts that this is the proud fulfilment of their being."

The general got to his feet.

"I should like to think that I shall take part in that war," he roared. "It would be a great honor for me, as an officer and a German."

Bredwitz jumped up angrily.

"God will never allow such a war to start!" he shouted.

"Our God has always been a Prussian God!" the general shouted back. For a moment he stared at the men about him. Then he raised his hands and went on, even more loudly than before.

"The Russians have four thousand fighter planes in the Arctic. The Americans have a garrison of forty thousand soldiers, armed with the most modern weapons in the world, stationed in the White Sea. Barely fifty miles away the Soviets have deployed twenty-five divisions. Off the coasts of Siberia they are training their submarines in atomic bombardment of the mainland, while other submarines carry out feints off the Pacific coast of the U.S.A. In America the greatest air raid exercises of all time are taking place. In Europe atomic artillery is ready. Everybody is arming and training and carrying out maneuvers, while I have to sit here and act the old soldier! But there is a stupendous task waiting for me! I should be given a command immediately! Today!" the general shouted. "God in heaven," he groaned, "you cannot betray your own creature! Give me back my career!"

Exhausted, he fell back into his armchair. My mouth was dry, and I swallowed a quick schnapps.

"The history of the German army," Bredwitz shouted, "is the history of generals who have cared more for a marshal's baton than for the life of their nation." He raised his arm and pointed at the general. "And there you see a living example of it."

Pandemonium broke loose. The former divisional chaplain threw a full glass of champagne in Bredwitz's face. The general was moaning loudly. He clutched his head with both hands.

"Oh, God!" he said.

Suddenly he bellowed, as a soldier will bellow when a shell splinter tears his entrails from his body. Then the noise changed to laughter, which grew louder and shriller, until suddenly it stopped.

We carried the general to the car. I drove along dark and narrow streets, across a bridge. Now we were in the country, and the road ran south. Alone upon a pile of stones stood a crucifix.

IN THE doctor's car were two male nurses from the asylum, with noncommittal faces. Like people who wash corpses, or prison guards. They took off their hats as they entered the general's house.

Upstairs a door banged. The general looked over the banisters. His eyes were flaming, and mad.

"God be with you, gentlemen," he said rustily.

Grinning awkwardly he made his way down the stairs.

"I knew that you would be coming," he mumbled at the men. "I knew you wouldn't leave me out in the cold."

He rubbed his hands together gleefully. He hurried excitedly across the hall. The men from the asylum exchanged rapid glances.

The general stared at them.

"You've come to offer me a command, haven't you?" he whispered. "I know, I know. And I'll accept it," he hissed.

He shuffled his feet and stared at the ceiling. He was unshaven and there were deep shadows under his eyes. Spittle dribbled from the corner of his mouth. Snot stuck to his jacket sleeve.

"Of course I'm prepared to take over my new duties immediately," he shouted and banged his chest enthusiastically with his fist. "Would you gentlemen be good enough to excuse me for a moment?"

In high excitement he ran up the stairs, to his study. Frenziedly he tore open cupboards and trunks. He stumbled about among the confusion of objects. He snatched piles of papers and books and threw them indiscriminately on the desk. "I'm only taking the bare essentials," he whispered, and scrabbled angrily at the maps upon the wall until they fell down. He grabbed his briefcase from the desk drawer and stuffed it full of papers, any papers. "The gentlemen in the hall are from the General Staff," he whispered significantly. His expression was that of a man imparting a well-kept and important secret.

His hands ran lovingly over the leather briefcase.

"In here are the basic documents which I need to arrange the war," he said, his eyes full of lust.

Then he began to urinate. His pupils were wide and fixed. He was grinning happily.

"A wonderful task awaits me!" he bawled. "A lovely job!" Urine spread across the carpet. Suddenly he drew himself up, pulling himself together. Gravely and proudly he came down the stairs. Step by step. As though he were on parade. I followed slowly behind.

There he goes, I thought, my old general. He's happy and contented. It won't be hard for him to believe his loony bin is the War Ministry. He'll never be bored. His briefcase is full of work to do. The general will settle down to his mighty plans and won't rest till they've been worked out in the minutest detail. He'll remember every little thing, tanks and soldiers, bombs and shells.

"Blessed Archangel Michael, patron saint of the German nation, and all saints, watch over this old warrior. Because he has the Knight's Cross with Oak leaves and Swords," I prayed.

The general marched down the last steps. He ran, gasping, through the hall, across the garden and down to the gate where the car was waiting. The men from the asylum hurried after him. The doctor sighed and took out his handkerchief.

"You have my heartfelt sympathy," he said to the general's daughter, by way of consolation. "Your father, whom we all respect so deeply, is suffering from manic-depressive insanity. It is the occupational malady of military men."

The general's daughter was crying.

IT WAS raining.

I walked through the cemetery. Along the path that led to the gate. Through its wrought-iron bars I saw the gleaming asphalt and the parked cars.

I hurried between dripping trees and damp graves, past rhododendrons and green bushes. Dead leaves lay along the path and there were muddy puddles among the washed clay. Gray clouds hung over the mountains, and all the colors were faded in the dull half-light.

In the crown of an oak tree, under the thick foliage, sat huddled a crow, soaked to the skin.